"Your Highness!" she said, surprised. "I did not think to see you so soon."

"Oh, Riona!" I cried. I could barely get the words out. "It's terrible—something dreadful has happened. The queen has—they are all swans! Oh, how could she?"

"Liam, bring water!" Riona called to her brother. To me, she said, "Now, begin again. I can't make sense of what you're saying."

I took the cup the boy offered me and drank. Then I said, a bit more calmly, "The queen has not sent my brothers to school. I think that she has cast a spell and changed them into swans. They swim on Heart Lake."

PRINCESS
of the
WILD SWANS

Diane Zahler

HARPER
An Imprint of HarperCollinsPublishers

Poem on p. 84 from "Swans" by Sara Teasdale, in Sara
Teasdale, *Rivers to the Sea* (New York: Macmillan, 1915),
http://www.gutenberg.org/files/442/442.txt.

Poem on p. 100–101 based on "The Wild Swans at Coole" by William Butler
Yeats, in *The Wild Swans at Coole, and Other Poems* (New York: Macmillan, 1919),
http://www.bartleby.com/148/1.html.

Poem on p. 169 from "The Song of Wandering Aengus" by William
Butler Yeats, in *The Wind Among the Reeds* (New York: J. Lane, 1899),
http://www.bartleby.com/146/9.html.

Princess of the Wild Swans

Library of Congress Cataloging-in-Publication Data
Zahler, Diane.
   Princess of the wild swans / Diane Zahler—1st ed.
       p. cm.
   Summary: Twelve-year old Princess Meriel must sew shirts from
stinging nettles in order to rescue her five older brothers from their evil
stepmother's spell lest they remain swans forever. Inspired by the Andersen
fairy tale, "The Wild Swans."
   ISBN 978-0-06-200495-6 (pbk.)
   [1. Fairy tales. 2. Princesses—Fiction. 3. Brothers and sisters—Fiction.
4. Witches—Fiction. 5. Stepmothers—Fiction. 6. Magic—Fiction.]
   I. Title
PZ8.Z17Pri 2012   2011019378
[Fic]—dc22   CIP
                                                                     AC

Typography by Erin Fitzsimmons
13 14 15 16 17   CG/OPM   10 9 8 7 6 5 4 3 2 1
❖
First paperback edition, 2013

For Phil—
MTLI

My grateful thanks to the following:
Maria Gomez and Barbara Lalicki, for their flawless editing
Shani Soloff, for being the ideal reader
Kathy Zahler, who created the perfect bookmarks
Stan and Jan Zahler, who have helped in every possible way
Ben Sicker, for believing in me (and putting me on Facebook!)
The members of Whine and Dine, whose support means more than I can say

CONTENTS

The Beginning:
And Who Appeared

I will not do it!" I cried, stamping my foot on the marble floor. "I will not, and you cannot make me!"

My governess, Mistress Tuileach, looked befuddled and weary, as she often did. She held out a needle threaded with gold thread, and I shook my head firmly.

"Your Highness, you must learn to sew a fine stitch," she pleaded. "All high-born ladies can sew."

I scowled. "But why? We do not make our own clothes—we have dressmakers for that. We don't hem our sheets or darn our stockings. There are servants for those chores. We simply sit beside a fire looking pretty and embroidering a useless pillow cover or handkerchief. And I will not do it!"

"It is what is done," said Mistress Tuileach helplessly, her high forehead creased in an anxious frown.

"Not by me," I insisted. "I have already spilled enough of my blood from fingers pricked by needles. You know I am hopeless at it. Instead I will take up a golden pen and finest parchment, as my brothers do, and practice writing and mathematics, and I will learn to shoot an arrow and feint with a sword."

Mistress Tuileach was scandalized. "Oh, Your Highness, no!" she implored. "Your father will dismiss me if you attempt such deeds. You already write and do sums quite well enough for a princess, and no lady would wield a sword! Your brothers may someday rule the kingdom, so they must know all manner of things. But you will be a wife and mother, and so must learn—"

"To sing? To play the lyre harp and dance the Rinnce Fada?" I stamped my foot again, wincing as the unforgiving marble bruised me through my thin leather slippers. "Even if I am to be a wife and mother, I may also be a queen, married to a king. Does a queen not need to know rhetoric and logic, and how to manage the household accounts? Should she not be able to ride and shoot with her nobles?"

I turned my back on my governess and walked to the window of the ladies' salon, where we stood arguing. To calm myself I took a deep breath of the warm autumn breeze that wafted in the open window, which extended from the floor of the room to its ceiling.

"And what king would have such a stubborn, uncultured girl for a wife?" Mistress Tuileach muttered under her breath. My hearing was uncommonly sharp, however, and I spun around in a fury, ready to dismiss her myself, though of course I had no power to do so.

At that moment, we both heard the sound of wheels on hard-packed earth. We were expecting no guests, for my father, the king, had been away on business for some weeks, so Mistress Tuileach and I both turned to the window to see who our visitors might be.

When I saw the high-stepping gray stallion far back behind a line of wooden wagons heading up the lane that led to our castle, I knew right away. "Father!" I called out, thrilled.

Without thinking I leaped through the open ground-floor window, hearing Mistress Tuileach scream behind me, "No, Princess Meriel! You will harm yourself!"

In fact, it was a rather longer drop to the ground than I had imagined, and it knocked the wind right out of me. I lay on the grass, stunned, trying to draw a breath. In a minute, though, I felt strong hands lifting me and looked up to see Cullan, the second-oldest of my five older brothers. His green eyes danced in his handsome face as he swung me to my feet.

"Are you running away from your governess or running to your father, Meriel?" he teased me.

"Both!" I said, brushing the grass off my linen over-dress. I frowned at the long streak of dirt on the hem. I knew I would hear from Mistress Tuileach about that.

"But look," Cullan said, pointing at the wagons. "Father must have bought everything he saw to be bringing home so much!"

Our father had a great love for finery and comfort and often purchased items abroad that we could not get in or around our own kingdom. Our home, Castle Rua, was from the outside a rough stone fortress like every other castle in the land. It had been built on the top of a tall hill overlooking fields and a blue lake that sparkled in the sunlight. In olden days, Castle Rua had been protection for the nearby town of Tiramore, and its people would take shelter there when enemies attacked. Now, under Father's wise rule, the town was large and prosperous, and our kingdom and those around it had been at peace for many years. Our castle was no longer needed as a stronghold.

Inside its stone walls, Father had put in long arched windows of clearest glass crafted in Coilin, floors of marble shipped across the sea from the mines of Tiafa, beautiful tapestries with scenes from ancient times woven on the great looms of Ardin. Even my governess had been brought from a far kingdom. Most noblewomen were taught the domestic arts by their mothers, but I had none to teach me, so Mistress Tuileach had arrived one day in a wagon along with a supply of silver plate.

Our personal items too were luxurious. My party dresses were made of silk and velvet, though most of the noblewomen and princesses I knew made do with linen, and my dancing shoes were trimmed with jewels. I once asked my youngest brother, Druce, how Father had become rich enough to buy such extravagances. Druce, whose knowledge of Latin was surpassed only by his skill with numbers, told me that after our mother's death ten years before, Father had diverted himself from his grief by amassing great wealth. I did not much care how he had done it, but I was very glad of it, for I did adore my butter-soft riding boots, my beautiful caramel-colored mare, and the warmth that constantly burning fires and thick tapestries brought to our drafty stone castle.

My other four brothers joined us on the grassy verge

that had once been a moat before Father had it filled in to prevent the odor and contagion of stale water. Aidan, the second-youngest, pushed his chestnut-colored curls from his eyes as he tried to see the end of the line of carts coming up the lane.

"There are a number of horses and riders," he observed. "I see Sir Paidin and Sir Brion—how many knights did Father take with him?"

"Four, I think," said my oldest brother, Darrock, the crown prince. His royal coronet, which he wore at all times, sparkled in the sun.

"There are five horses besides Father's," Aidan said. "Perhaps, Meriel, Father has brought home a husband for you!"

I swatted at him, and he danced away, laughing. I always pretended to be annoyed when my brothers teased me, but in truth I loved it, for they so seldom seemed even to notice me. Most days they were too busy with their schooling and their sports. Oh, how I envied them, out in the fresh air or learning in the great library with their tutor! They hunted, practiced sword-play, rode for hours, and had lessons in all the seven liberal arts. Darrock had extra lessons as well to pre-pare him for his duties as crown prince. Druce could hardly ever be torn from his books nor Baird from his music, while Cullan had a habit of disappearing for hours at a time, only to return flushed and smelling sweetly of someone's lilac or rosewater scent. So unless I was shouting in a tantrum, it was rare that I got more than a moment of my brothers' attention.

Now we all six stood together and watched as the figures on horseback made their way past the laden wagons and trotted up the lane. There were Sir Paidin and Sir Brion, as Aidan had said, and Lords Saran and Osan. But another mount pranced beside Father's, and as they came closer I was startled to see that the rider was not a knight but a woman.

"Who," I said, pointing rudely, "is *that*?"

She sat on her black horse elegantly, with a straight back and a firm grip, and we could see that she was tall and slim, with a long, slender neck. Her dress, under her velvet cloak, was rich green satin. Her face was veiled, but her dark hair blew in the breeze as she cantered with Father up to the massive door in the wall that enclosed the castle forecourt. The knights had already dismounted and stood ready to help the lady down. When she reached the door, she brushed them aside and slid from her horse with uncommon grace. Then she lifted her veil.

My brothers made not a sound, though Cullan's hand on my shoulder tightened its grip enough to make me wince, but I gasped to see the beauty of her face.

Her skin was as pale as moonlight, unflushed from her ride, her lips full and rosy. Her arched brows framed dark eyes that immediately fastened on the six of us. She betrayed no emotion at all.

Father dismounted then, and Darrock strode to greet him. "Your Majesty," he said formally, "welcome home. We have missed you sorely."

"My son," Father said, and they grasped each other by the forearm. Then I could wait no longer but pushed my brother aside and leaped into my father's arms, nearly knocking him over.

"Father!" I cried. "We did not expect you. I am so glad you're home!"

"Child," Father said reprovingly, "this is not ladylike behavior. You must restrain yourself. Has your governess taught you nothing?" But his voice was warm, and his arms were tight around me. He kissed my cheek, his beard rough against my skin. At last I loosened my hold on him, and he greeted my other brothers: Cullan bowed deeply, sweeping off his cap with grace, Baird and Aidan mimicked Darrock's formal welcome, and Druce bobbed his head, his serious face creased in a smile. The knights bowed to us as well and began motioning the wagon drivers into the forecourt to begin unloading the goods that Father had brought.

Then the woman cleared her throat delicately, and

Father turned to her, looking somewhat abashed.

"Forgive me, my dear," he said, taking her hand. My eyes widened when I saw this, but before I could say anything, Father went on: "In the excitement, I have quite forgotten my manners. These are my children: Darrock, my eldest son, who is twenty-two, and Cullan, Baird, Aidan, and Druce, each two years younger. And this little minx is my daughter and the baby of the family, the princess Meriel."

The woman looked closely at us then. I could see something in her eyes that made me uneasy. She seemed both surprised and displeased by us, and I wondered briefly if the dirt on my dress was the cause. Though I admired her clothes and horsemanship, I felt an instant dislike for her. I could not say why, but I knew my feeling was reciprocated. Still, I curtsied deeply, and my brothers bowed, and then my father said, "Children, this is the lady Orianna. Come and welcome my queen, your new mother."

2

The Enchantment:
And Who Disappeared

It took the rest of the day and most of that evening to move the lady Orianna's belongings into the castle. The wagon drivers were the queen's own guards—in very elegant red and gold livery—and they and the castle guards were put to work unloading. The wagons were filled with her possessions: her gowns and doeskin shoes, her nightdresses and furred cloaks and jewels. She even brought her own furniture, ornately carved pieces with satiny cushions to displace the chairs and benches that Father had collected since our mother's death.

I saw Ogan, the youngest of our guards, struggling to lift an enormous gilt mirror. He was the only one of the guards I really knew; he often joined Aidan in lawn tennis or other sports that needed a partner. Once, years ago, Ogan had rescued me when I was stuck climbing a tree, and he had never mentioned the humiliating incident to anyone. In return, I always smiled at him when I passed. Now he met my eyes as he staggered by with the mirror, but I was too distressed to spare him even a nod.

The kitchen staff flew into a frenzy of preparation for an elaborate welcome-home meal. Before dinner my brothers gathered in the room that had been our nursery when we were small. It was still the place in the castle where we felt most at home. Late-afternoon sunlight streamed across the faded carpet, and toys from days long past lined the shelves along one wall. I sat in the corner, making myself very small and quiet. I was quite skilled at this, though some might say I was better at making a large noise. But I loved to sit and listen to my brothers talk amongst themselves, and if they noticed me, they would usually send me away.

"She is uncommonly pretty," Cullan said as he draped himself along a settee, his boots kicked off.

"Pretty? I would say beautiful," Aidan corrected him, pushing Cullan aside so he too could sit.

"But should we speak of our new mother that way?" Cullan asked teasingly. "Though I doubt she is five years older than Darrock, so perhaps we should not call her mother."

Baird perched on a stool and strummed his lute. He began to sing:

"The black swan bends her graceful neck
And grooms herself with care;
Her onyx eyes are fathomless,
Her beak could rend and tear."

I looked at him sharply. A black swan—that described her perfectly, with her long neck and dark hair.

"Did you see Father's face when he looked at her? And the ruby ring he has given her?" Druce asked, closing his book. "He seems quite in her thrall. She has done her work very quickly."

"Oh, she is not so bad!" Cullan protested.

"I don't know," Druce reflected. "There is something strange about her . . . she reminds me just a little of your new friend Riona."

I perked up. I had not heard of Riona. I knew Cullan was spending time with someone, and I knew it was a girl, for it was always a girl. Few could resist my brother's handsome face and wit, and though he broke at least one heart a month, he was so very charming that he rarely left anger in his wake.

"Are you saying our new mother is a witch?" Cullan inquired, a lazy smile on his lips.

"Is Riona a witch, then?" asked Aidan with great interest, rolling a wooden ball across the carpet. "You should beware, brother, or she will snare you in a love spell!"

"Don't speak ill of Riona," Cullan said lightly, but there was a warning in his tone. I was surprised, for usually he paid no mind to his brothers' jokes about his female conquests.

"Perhaps that is what happened to Father—a love spell," Druce suggested.

"That may be the sort of thing that happens in the books you read, but I don't think the new queen needs magic to ensnare a man," Cullan pointed out. "Her face alone casts a spell that any man would have trouble resisting—much less a man who has been wifeless these ten years!"

I could not restrain myself any longer. "I don't like her," I burst out.

All five brothers turned to stare at me.

"Shouldn't you be dressing for dinner, Meriel?" Darrock scolded. "I'm sure Mistress Tuileach is looking for you."

"But why don't you like her?" Cullan asked me, interested. "You've barely met."

"I don't know," I admitted. "It's as Druce said—there is something about her. Her eyes, or her manner, or the way she looked at us. She makes me uneasy."

"Ah," said Aidan, grinning. "You are used to being the only hen in the flock. You are jealous of sharing your position!"

"That is not it at all!" I snapped, but the boys were laughing now, and I got up and stormed out of the nursery, annoyed as only my brothers—and perhaps a little taste of truth—could make me.

Dinner was a strange and solemn meal. The queen, dressed in a gown of deep red that set off her dark beauty, sat at Father's right hand, in Darrock's usual place. Darrock was visibly displeased at the change. The mirror I had seen Ogan carry had been hung at one end of the long room, and I noted with irritation that it was positioned so that Lady Orianna could see her reflection as she sat at the table.

With every failure of manners—and there were many, for we were used to a family dinner without much ceremony—her full lips drew into a thin line that judged us more severely than words could have. At one point, between the fish and the fowl, she turned to Father and said, "Gearalt, my dearest, when you said you had children, I did not imagine five boys!" Her words sounded playful, but she did not smile.

"And a girl," I piped up before I could stop myself. Her dark gaze swung to me and I felt its chill, but I stuck out my chin and did not shrink away.

"How did you meet Lady Orianna, Father?" Cullan inquired to change the subject, kicking me under the table.

"There was a ball in Ardin," Father told us, his eyes dreamy. "I had not planned to go, but Lord Breasal insisted, and glad I was when I arrived! The lady Orianna was the first thing I saw, and I saw nothing else that whole evening."

"Ever since," said Lady Orianna in a silken voice, "we have been inseparable. We married before the month was out."

"Did you not think to write to us and let us know, Father?" Darrock asked. "We could have prepared a better welcome for you both."

Father looked a little bemused. "It all happened so quickly. . . ," he murmured.

"Well, then, a toast to you," said Darrock, lifting his goblet. "To your marriage—may it be long and full of joy." But his tone was flat as he said it, and the clink of goblets touched together sounded harsh to me.

Late that night, I was awakened by the sound of a voice

raised in anger. I had slept in a room next to Father's since Mother died, for as a small child I was plagued with night terrors and only Father could comfort me. Though the castle walls were thick, my clothes closet backed on his, and when my closet doors were open I could hear conversations in his room. Many were the times I had opened the doors to listen to Father dispensing advice or reprimands to my brothers.

I tumbled out of bed and crept into my closet, pressing my ear against the wall.

"How could you keep such a thing from me?" I heard Lady Orianna demand in a tone of great indignation. "You told me of your daughter, but five boys—was this a secret you thought I somehow would not learn?"

"My love, I do not understand," Father responded, sounding bewildered. "I did not say anything because I did not think it would matter."

"You are simpleminded, then," Lady Orianna said bitterly. "Only the male children can grow up to rule in your kingdom, so of course your sons matter to me. What of our own children? If I should find myself with child and give you a son, he will never be king!"

Father's reply was low and measured, and I had to strain to hear it. "No, Orianna, should that happy event occur, our child could not be king. There are five princes who would be ahead of him in the succession.

But he would be a prince of the realm, and I would love him as I do my other children."

There was a silence, and then Lady Orianna said, "I am sorry, my dear. Of course you would love our child. You are quite right—that is what matters. I do not know what I was thinking. Forgive me—the strain of our long journey has exhausted me and made me speak foolishly." Her voice was suddenly sweet, and it made my skin crawl.

"You must rest, my love," Father said fondly, and then all was quiet.

I did not sleep again that night but lay replaying the conversation in my mind, and in the morning I went straight to Darrock. He had been rising early each morning to meet with advisors and see to Father's business while he was away. I found him in the dining hall, where he was breakfasting on smoked fish and dark bread and tea, a pile of papers to be read and signed already stacked before him.

"Meriel!" Darrock said in surprise, for I rarely woke before nine and usually ate breakfast with Mistress Tuileach. "You are about early this morning. Here, have some bread and jam."

"I am not hungry. I need to tell you something," I said emphatically, and I related what I had overheard between Father and Lady Orianna. Beneath his golden coronet, Darrock's brow creased. I could see that my tale disturbed him.

"I think Druce might be right," I told him. "I think the lady has enchanted Father. We must do something!"

Darrock sighed. "She is not a witch, Meriel," he assured me. "She is simply a young and beautiful woman with whom our father has fallen in love. Of course she wants any male child she bears to rule—but that cannot be. It sounds as if Father has made that quite clear."

"But—," I began, agitated.

"Meriel, I have work I must do. She is your step-mother, and there is nothing to be done about it. You must learn to get along with her."

"But. . . ," I said again, trailing off when I saw that Darrock's attention had already turned from me to the papers before him. Frustrated, I left the dining hall and went in search of my other brothers. As I came to the front entryway, I saw that Lady Orianna had placed her own guards, in their dark red uniforms with gold buttons and epaulets, at the door. They crossed their lances before me, blocking my way, and I glared at them, furious.

"Make way for me," I ordered. "Do you not know who I am?"

"You are the princess Meriel," one of the guards replied carelessly. I noted his drooping black mustache and thought that he looked more like a fool than a guard.

"I am, and you must let me pass," I said.

"The queen has commanded that you must tell us where you are going," the mustached guard informed me. My rage boiled over.

"How dare you!" I cried out. "She cannot tell me what to do! Now, get out of my way, you scurvy villain!"

There were footsteps behind me, and then I felt a hand on my shoulder, gripping it hard. It was the lady Orianna, I could tell without turning around. Her scent, of spice and sandalwood and something strange and musky, announced her.

"Meriel, it is for your own safety," she said in a gentle voice. "I have seen that you are free to come and go as you please, and that is not proper for a princess. You have only to tell the guards where you are going, so we are not made anxious over your whereabouts."

I thought about refusing, but I did not want to antagonize her overmuch—not yet, at any rate. "I am going to the stables to see my brother," I said through gritted teeth.

"There!" she said with a little laugh. "That was not

hard, was it?" I shrugged her hand off my shoulder and darted under the guards' lances as they raised them, breaking into a run as soon as I guessed she had turned away.

In the gardens I slowed, noticing the groundsmen trimming back the roses and preparing the flowerbeds for the cold weather to come. I strode down the gravel footpath past the little pond filled with water lilies and fish both gold and spotted, past the fountain in the shape of a dolphin spouting, past hedges trimmed into shapes of animals—a tiger, an elephant, and my favorite, a unicorn. On the far side of the hedges, I came to the stables, where I found Aidan preparing to ride out for the day. Baird was with him, having been pried from his music for the outing. They listened to me, their horses prancing eagerly, and they too had little patience with what I had to say.

"Leave it be, Meriel," Baird advised me.

Aidan added, "You must convince the new queen what fine fellows we are, so she does not kill us off one by one to free the throne for her own child!" He and Baird laughed loud and long at the joke, but I felt quite frantic. To me such an act did not seem completely impossible.

I went back, passing by the guards without meeting their eyes, and climbed the great marble staircase to the library. There, as usual, was Druce, who sat at a polished wooden table piled with books, declining Latin verbs to himself in a low voice. He held up his hand to silence me when I entered and finished: "*Incantabam, incantarem, incantabo.*" When I told him my fears, he laughed too.

"Oh, Meriel, you are so dramatic!" he exclaimed, his lip stained with ink where he chewed on his pen nib. "You mustn't take what I said yesterday seriously. I promise you, she is no threat to us. She is just a woman whose plans for her future have been foiled. Stay out of her way, and she will get over it."

Finally I climbed up one more flight of stairs to the royal bedchambers and went to Cullan, still asleep in a tangle of bedclothes in his darkened room. I threw open the long linen drapes, and the sun streamed in across his bed.

"What is it?" he moaned, covering his head with a pillow. "Is that you, Meriel? Do go away, please."

"I will not," I said firmly, and proceeded to relate to him the night's conversation and our brothers' reactions. By the time I was finished, he was more or less awake, and his green eyes were bright and interested.

"Those are not the words of a happy bride," he observed, stretching long and motioning me to perch beside him.

"No indeed," I agreed. "I am sure she has enchanted Father in some way, as Druce said."

Cullan shook his head. "What you overheard is certainly no proof of witchcraft or wicked intentions."

I had to admit that he was right—Lady Orianna's words were not evil in themselves. "I know that," I said. "But there is something strange about her, don't you think?"

"It is not so strange that a beautiful young woman marries an older, wealthy, powerful man," Cullan pointed out. "In fact, it is pretty much the way of the world."

I pouted. "Well, I plan to watch her closely. And if I see anything that points to . . . well, anything out of the ordinary—"

"If you do," Cullan assured me, "I will bring my friend Riona to meet her. Like can recognize like, I have heard—she will be able to tell if Lady Orianna has dark powers or only dark desires."

"Will you really?" I said excitedly, bouncing on the bed. "I should like very much to meet Riona! Could you bring her today? Please?"

"I just told you I would bring her to the castle if you found anything suspicious," Cullan said, his patience used up. "Now give me some peace. It's barely dawn, and your bouncing makes my head ache."

It was nearly noon by this time, but I left smiling. On my way out, I snatched a scone from the tray that held Cullan's breakfast, long since gone cold, and ate it as I went back to my room. Now I had a plan. I had only to watch and wait.

The trouble was, there seemed nothing to see. Lady Orianna spent the day overseeing the unpacking of her vast store of trunks and boxes. From behind doors and around corners, I watched in amazement as clothes in marvelous colors and luxurious fabrics were brushed and hung. Her slippery-cushioned chairs and divans replaced our own elegant but comfortable pieces, which went home with Sir Paidin, Sir Brion, and other pleased courtiers. I fumed when I saw that an enormous painting of the new queen, bright and glittering in a silver gown, had taken the place of my mother's portrait in the throne room.

I constantly had to dodge out of sight or out of the way as Lady Orianna bustled through the castle, changing the position of this or that painting, vase, or mirror. Once, when I did not move quickly enough, she brushed me aside as if I were a bothersome pup, murmuring, "Do get out of the way, child. I am surpassing busy."

Oh, how that vexed me! It was the same thing my brothers—and even Father—always said to me. I had never much wanted a new mother, but I had always assumed that if Father were to remarry, his new wife would at least be kind to me. Indulgent, even, as I had been motherless for so long. But Lady Orianna seemed determined to take for herself what little attention my father bestowed on me. Every time that day that I found a moment to be with Father, she somehow knew it and would appear to ask for advice on the placement of a vase or the menu for dinner. Father would turn to her, his face lighting up like a beacon, and I would be utterly forgotten. By day's end I thoroughly despised her.

I went back to Cullan's room just before I went to bed. He was readying himself to go out for the evening, smoothing his reddish-brown curls before a mirror. Clothes were strewn about, and a row of polished boots, from which he had obviously chosen the gleaming pair he wore, stood at attention by the hearth.

"Ah, Meriel," he said, smiling distractedly at me as he adjusted his embroidered tunic. "How goes the witch hunt?"

"It is surely the truth that she is a witch," I told him. "Each time I tried to talk with Father, she appeared as if by magic. Clearly she does not want us to speak. She fears being discovered."

Cullan looked at me closely then, and I could see a

gentleness in his gaze that he, my most ironic brother, did not usually show.

"It is to be expected, Sister," he said kindly. "They are newlyweds, and she wishes to be with him. You must step aside for now."

His words enraged me. "I am not jealous of her!" I shouted, feeling unwelcome tears press behind my eyes. I willed them back. "She is a witch and I know it! You promised to bring Riona here to prove it!"

Cullan sighed and picked up his cloak. "Very well, Meriel. If it will set your mind at ease, I shall ask Riona to come tomorrow."

"Do you promise?" I demanded.

"Yes, I promise," he said, his tone a little irritated now. "I am late—I must go. Behave yourself when I am gone!"

"And you too," I said automatically, our customary parting words.

I left the room, and in the hall I saw Lady Orianna, straightening yet another new portrait. She paid no mind to me, and I just as pointedly ignored her as I ran past her to my bedchamber. I did not usually like to spend much time there, but just now it seemed a haven from all the unpleasant changes that were transforming the rest of the castle. It was a pretty place, sunny and bright in daytime and cozy at night, with lacy curtains and bedspread, a glass-topped dressing table, and flowered carpets. Though I would not have chosen to decorate it so daintily, I knew my mother had picked the furnishings when I was but a baby, so I did not mind them as much as I might have.

I let Mistress Tuileach find me there. I had escaped her clutches all day with my stealth and spying, and she was not pleased.

"You will be behind in your lessons," she scolded, brushing my unruly hair smooth as I sat before the dressing table, buttoning my nightdress.

"Behind what?" I asked belligerently, and she sighed much as Cullan had done.

"Oh, child, you are as prickly as a nettle," she said sadly.

I turned to her then, repentant. "I don't mean to be, Mistress Tuileach, truly. I will be better tomorrow."

"Good," she said, "for nettles are not very pleasant to hug." Then, to my shock, she leaned down and gave me a brief squeeze, her arms warm and welcoming around me. She had never embraced me before. I hugged her back, surprised and pleased, crawled into bed, and fell asleep with a smile on my face.

And in the morning when I woke, my brothers, all five, were gone.

3

The Swans:
And Where They Swam

T hey are gone? What do you mean, gone?"
I asked Mistress Tuileach numbly. She
had been dispatched to give me the news,
for obviously Father feared a tantrum or
worse from me on hearing it. But I was too distraught
to do anything but stare at my governess as she spoke.

"They have been sent to school," Mistress Tuileach
reported, watching me anxiously. She paused a moment
and added, "They must have left before dawn, for I did
not see them go."

"School? But they have a tutor. And Darrock is

surely too old for school—Cullan too!" I protested.

"It is a special school, the queen says. All the noble boys and princes from her kingdom go there to be trained for their roles in manhood. Your brothers will learn the ways of kings there, she says. And it seems that your father agrees."

"But . . . ," I said, my voice trailing off. *The queen says!* Of course it was Lady Orianna's doing. "It did not take her long," I muttered.

"What did you say, child?" Mistress Tuileach asked, laying out my clothes for the day. She darted little glances at me, waiting, no doubt, for an outburst. But my heart was like a nut in my chest, small and dark and hard, and I could not tell whether I felt anger or despair.

"Nothing," I said, and I dressed quietly, my mind racing. Around my neck I fastened the necklace I always wore, a small sapphire on a gold chain that Cullan had given me for my last name day. It was very precious to me.

"Mistress Tuileach," I said as I sat before the mirror so she could brush and braid my hair, "how long will they be at school? Will they come home for visits?"

"I do not know," Mistress Tuileach replied, tying a green ribbon on my braid to match my overdress.

"There, the ribbon brings out the green in your eyes."

I stared at my reflection without seeing it. I did not care about the color of my eyes. "I think they will not visit," I said, half to myself. "I think we will not see them at all."

"Try to eat a little breakfast, Your Highness," Mistress Tuileach urged, and I took a slice of bread from the tray Mistress Tuileach had brought and buttered it. But I knew I could not force it past the lump in my throat, so I laid it back on the plate.

"I am going for a walk," I said.

"Your father told me that the queen does not want you wandering about as you have in the past. And it will rain, I believe," my governess said. I ignored her words about Lady Orianna and went to the closet to pull out my boots. For once, Mistress Tuileach did not nag me to stay and practice my singing or stitching, but let me go in silence.

I slipped through the halls and down to the cellars, where there was a side door often left unguarded. Now, however, there was a man in red livery standing before it, and my heart sank. Then I realized it was not one of the queen's men but our own guard Ogan, dressed in the same uniform as Lady Orianna's guards. I marched up to him.

"I am going for a walk," I announced confidently, although I was not sure whether he would let me pass.

He gazed at me thoughtfully, then looked around to make sure no one observed us and stood aside. I slipped past him, bowing my head in a way that I hoped conveyed thanks, and dodged behind bushes until I was sure I was far enough from the castle to walk on the lane.

As I strode along under lowering clouds, I was entirely lost in my own dark thoughts. I had no idea what to think of Father. It seemed a terrible betrayal, to send away his sons at his wife's insistence. I knew that before the lady Orianna had entered his life, he would never have dreamed of doing such a thing, and I was angry at him in a way I never had been before. I held silent conversations of blame and accusation with him in my mind, so absorbed that I nearly collided with a girl hurrying past me.

"Excuse me, milady," the girl said, and I nodded distractedly. Then she spoke again. "Princess Meriel? Is that you?"

I turned to look at her, awakened from my reverie. She was very pretty, perhaps seventeen or eighteen years old, with long dark curls, deep blue eyes, and vividly flushed cheeks and lips. She wore an undyed linen overdress and wooden shoes, and I marked her for the daughter of a tradesman. But I was wrong.

"I am Riona, your brother Cullan's friend," she said. She smiled at me, making her face even lovelier. Without warning, in the warmth of that smile, I burst into tears.

Immediately she was all concern. "Oh, Your Highness!" she exclaimed, pulling a rather coarse handkerchief from her dress pocket. "Whatever is wrong? Oh please, don't cry! Here, wipe your tears— come sit with me." She led me to a fallen log beside the lane, and I mopped my face with the rough cloth, trying to control myself. She patted my shoulder and murmured soothing words, and at last my sobs stopped. I blew my nose.

"I have ruined your handkerchief," I said shakily.

"It was not much to begin with," she assured me. "I am terrible at embroidery—see the uneven stitches?"

I looked, and almost had to smile. "You are very nearly as bad as I am," I observed, and Riona laughed.

"Now, will you tell me what is wrong? Has your wicked brother teased you past all enduring?"

At the mention of Cullan, tears threatened again, but I took a deep breath and said, "I wish he could tease me. I wish he would tease me until I screamed. But he is gone. They are all gone."

Her eyes widened in alarm. "Gone! But where? Why?"

"The new queen has sent them off to school. I don't know where," I answered, my voice trembling.

Riona looked at me sharply. "To school? But Cullan said nothing to me! Oh, that is very strange, and very sudden." I could see she was now quite distressed, and I wondered how strong her feelings were for my brother.

"Did Cullan tell you what I fear about the queen?" I asked.

She nodded. "That is why I was coming to you. He said you wanted me to see her. To see if I could tell. . . ."

"Yes!" I said. "Can you? Will you? I am so afraid that she will somehow keep my brothers from returning. I need to know what she's capable of doing."

"I can try," Riona replied, rising from the log and brushing off her skirt. "But even if I am able to tell what she is, I don't know what I can do for you, or for your brothers. I am only half a witch, you see, though it is on my mother's side."

"Is that good, to be a witch on your mother's side?" I inquired, rising as well. We started back up the lane as a fine misty rain began to fall.

"It gives me more power, as a woman myself," she explained. "When only one parent is a witch, it is strongest in the children of the same sex. But I have not done much with my inheritance. I use it mostly for healing, with the herbs from my garden and wild plants from the woods."

"Perhaps you could teach me a little of your art," I said, surprising myself with the suggestion. I scurried to keep up with her, for her legs were long and she moved quickly.

She looked at me sidelong. "I did not think you liked to study," she said with a small smile.

I scowled. "Did Cullan tell you that? It's not true, not at all. I don't like to learn the things that Father and my governess believe a lady should know—they are all so boring! But I should love to learn something useful, and healing sounds very useful indeed."

Riona smiled again. "Cullan thinks you can do anything you set your mind to doing," she told me. "He has great confidence in you."

"Does he?" I asked breathlessly. "Really?" The thought warmed me through, and I suddenly felt very much better as we hurried to get to the castle before the rain began in earnest.

"I think I should probably not introduce you to the queen," I said to Riona as we tried to neaten our clothes. I felt a little awkward. "She might find it . . . odd if I did."

Riona laughed and twirled around, her damp

overdress flapping about her. "Am I not dressed finely enough for her?"

I giggled. "She is very elegant. I can't imagine that she would greet anyone wearing muddy shoes—or wearing wooden shoes at all, for that matter." Immediately I realized how rude I sounded, but Riona did not seem to mind. In fact, she was not offended at all, and I found that I was beginning to like her very much.

"I can try to view her from a distance," she said, pulling up the hood of her cloak so that I could barely see her face. We went back to the door where I had exited, and Ogan let us in after making certain the way was clear. I led Riona up the stairs and through the long halls, looking for the lady Orianna. She was not in any of the staterooms, nor upstairs in her bedchamber. We descended to the vast kitchen, and as we went down the stairs I heard her giving complicated and exacting instructions to the cook for a formal dinner. I could tell, from the number of courses and quantities she laid out, that she meant to invite many lords and ladies.

Riona and I lurked behind a door, trying hard to glimpse the queen's face, but her back was to us. When at last she had finished giving orders, she spun around more quickly than we expected, catching us by surprise. She frowned at me.

"Meriel, what are you doing down here?" she asked,

taking in my rain-spattered dress. Then she turned to Riona, who pushed back her hood. Her gaze met Lady Orianna's. I watched the queen's face carefully. Her eyes narrowed as Riona looked long at her, and color rose in the queen's cheeks, the first flush I had seen on her pale skin.

"Who is this girl?" she demanded, turning back to me.

Caught off guard, I stammered, "A—a new maid. A kitchen maid. I was showing her where to go."

"I did not approve a new maid," Lady Orianna said imperiously.

I improvised wildly. "She was hired before you came, but she could not start right away."

Lady Orianna glanced again at Riona and then turned back to me, shaking her head. "I do not want her here." Then to Riona she said, "You are dismissed." Riona pulled her hood up again and nodded meekly.

"And you will go to your room," Lady Orianna said to me. "I am sure that your governess is looking for you."

I curtsied. "Yes, milady," I said in what I hoped was a humble voice, though my fists were clenched. Riona and I turned and ran to the cellar stairs, down them, and along the hall to the side door. Ogan stood aside once more.

"I must go," Riona hissed. "You were right. She knows what I am, and I know what she is. She must not see me again. Come to me at my home when you can. Take the second right-hand path before town. Goodbye!"

"Farewell," I whispered, pushing the heavy door open. She slipped through it into the rain-soaked afternoon and was gone.

The next day I was desperate to get out to see Riona, but Mistress Tuileach waylaid me and insisted I spend time practicing the art of the tea service. In the ladies' salon I paced impatiently as she showed me the proper way to pour. I spilled the tea, of course, for my hand shook with urgency, and I knocked over the milk and scattered the sugar onto the table as well. Finally Mistress Tuileach threw up her hands.

"Begone, child!" she exclaimed. "You are more trouble than you are worth." I snatched up my cloak, surprised that she would let me leave against the queen's orders. As I left the room she called after me, "Be sure you are back before sundown. The queen expects you at her dinner and ball tonight!"

I turned back. "A ball? She is giving a ball? But she has only just arrived!"

Mistress Tuileach nodded. "I believe that she

planned it after her wedding in Ardin. It is to be her welcoming party."

Without replying I ran down to the cellar. Ogan stood at attention by the door, and I asked, "Will you let me pass?"

"I will, Your Highness, for your brothers' sake," he said, and I looked at him sharply. Then I recalled the many times he'd played tennis with Aidan and hunted with Cullan. He too must be distressed that they were gone. I nodded, ducked once more under Ogan's raised lance, pushed open the door, and dashed down the lane toward town.

The lane curved at the foot of the hill on which our castle perched. The fields below were bright with autumn green and gold. About a mile away was Tiramore, the largest town in the kingdom, its rooftops red tiled and its chimneys puffing smoke.

Off to the right I could see the shimmer of blue water under sunny skies—Heart Lake, so named for its shape, like a child's cutout for St. Valentine's Day. It was fed by a spring that some said bubbled up from the lands of Faerie below the earth. Mist hovered over the water on its narrow, far side, never burning off even on the hottest, sunniest day. People were always telling of glimpses of strange beasts or magical bonfires there, though neither bone nor burnt offering ever remained to prove the rumors true. Cullan scoffed at these stories and often wooed girls at picnics on its shores, claiming that the lake's shape was a natural invitation to romance. I had never believed the tales either, so I decided to take the footpath that skirted the lake, for it was a shortcut to Tiramore.

When I reached the lake, I saw the ducks and geese that often swam upon it, looking for water plants or insects to eat and raising their babies in the weeds at the water's edge. There was also a flock of swans, which I had not seen there before. White, serene, majestic, they glided on the surface and were reflected in the water below, so it seemed almost that there were ten swans swimming rather than five.

The path came near to the lake where the swans floated. As I approached the place where path and water were closest, a most peculiar thing happened. One of the swans reared back until it was almost standing on the water and began to beat its wings wildly. The sight was so unexpected, the clamor so loud, that I stopped in my tracks and stared. One by one, the other swans followed suit, until there were five swans upright on the water's surface, flapping their wings with a noise like thunder. They were very beautiful and very fierce, and I stood motionless, afraid to continue past them.

At last they stopped flapping and lowered themselves to the water again. Carefully I started walking, but one of the birds paddled to the lake's edge and pulled itself onto the land. Awkwardly it waddled to the path in front of me, blocking my passage.

I had heard that swans could be foul tempered, even violent, so I backed away. The bird followed me. I backed still farther, faster, as the swan came at me. My shoe caught on a root and I fell to the ground, and without warning the swan extended its long neck, nipped hard, and with its sharp beak pulled off my necklace.

"Give that back!" I cried, incensed. The swan's head moved from side to side, almost as if it were saying no. "It was a gift from my brother! I will have it back!"

I put out my hand, and much to my amazement, the swan gently lowered the necklace into my palm. Confused, I looked into its eyes.

"Are you someone's pet?" I asked it. In reply, the swan laid its head on my arm. Hesitantly I stroked it, and the swan stretched its neck in a way that suddenly reminded me of Cullan stretching in his bed two mornings before, when I had wakened him. *No*, I thought, *it cannot be so.* But I asked anyway.

"Are you . . . can you be Cullan?"

In answer, the swan laid its head on my arm again and looked up at me. Its eyes were green, not black, as other swans' eyes were, and they danced with a light I knew well. Indeed, there was no doubt about it. They were my brother Cullan's eyes.

The Ball:
And What Was Learned

I ran then, as fast as I could, my heart hammering in my chest. Past the lake, through the meadow, down the path to where it rejoined the lane outside town. I skimmed past the first turnoff on the lane and took the second, as Riona had instructed. My thoughts skittered crazily, but my feet remembered her directions.

The path led through a small wood and then emerged into another meadow, dead-ending at a little stone thatch-roofed cottage. I hammered on the front door, gasping for air.

The door was opened by a dark-haired, blue-eyed boy about my age who looked vaguely familiar. He stared at me as I stood disheveled and out of breath.

"Oh," I panted, "this must be the wrong place. I am looking for Riona."

"Princess Meriel?" the boy said in a tone of disbelief.

"Yes, yes," I replied impatiently. "Do you know Riona? Does she live nearby?"

"She lives here," the boy said, motioning me to enter. "I'm her brother, Liam. I treat the horses and dogs at the castle when they are ailing." He paused, and I wondered if he thought that I should recognize him, or feel embarrassed that I did not. I waited, and finally he said, "Riona is in the back, tending her plants. What—?"

But I had already pushed past him and dashed through the tiny house to the back, where the open top half of a Dutch door revealed an enormous garden. There were raised boxes of herbs in front, and behind them were plants and flowers of all sorts. It was not at all like the elaborate, manicured garden we had at Castle Rua, with its boxwood hedges trimmed in topiary shapes and banks of roses in carefully chosen shades of pink. The flowers here looked like wildflowers to

me, but it was clear that they had been carefully cultivated. Their colors blended together in a vivid mix that
somehow excited and soothed the eye at the same time.

I could see Riona bent over one of the herb boxes,
and I shoved open the bottom part of the door and ran
out to her. At my approach she looked up, shading her
eyes against the sun with her hand.

"Your Highness!" she said, surprised. "I did not
think to see you so soon."

"Oh, Riona!" I cried. I could barely get the words
out. "It's terrible—something dreadful has happened.
The queen has—they are all swans! Oh, how could she?"

"Slow down," Riona urged me. She rose and led me
to a little stone bench. On the back of the bench a crow
perched, and to my surprise it did not move when I sat
to catch my breath. It stared at me with a single beady
eye; its other eye was missing.

"Liam, bring water!" Riona called to her brother. To
me, she said, "Now, begin again. I can't make sense of
what you're saying."

I took the cup the boy offered me and drank. Then
I said, a bit more calmly, "The queen has not sent my
brothers to school. I think that she has cast a spell and
changed them into swans. They swim on Heart Lake."

Riona stared at me, and I feared she might laugh at

such a wild pronouncement, for it sounded quite daft even to me. But she did not laugh. Her expression was filled with dismay. Even the boy looked very serious.

"That is a cruel enchantment," he observed. "What did they do to anger her?"

"They existed!" I snapped, focusing my rage at him. The crow moved from foot to foot, uneasy at my tone. "She wanted them out of the way for good—and this is how she has done it!"

"I'm sorry," the boy said, a little abashed. "I didn't know."

Riona made a visible effort to shake off her distress. "We should go to see them," she decided, leading me back through the house to the front door. She pulled a cloak from a peg on the wall and handed another to her brother. "I can judge then what might be done."

"Can you break such a spell?" I asked her as we started back up the path.

"I doubt it," she admitted. "Not by myself. But that doesn't mean the spell cannot be broken. I just have to find out how."

When we reached the lake, I could see the swans, across the water from us now. *Perhaps,* I thought desperately, *they are actually just birds like any other birds. Perhaps I was wrong.* But I could see my brothers in them all too well. The swan that I guessed was Darrock swam stiffly upright, patrolling the edges of the lake. The Aidan swan paddled in circles and figure eights, displaying his agility. The Baird swan stopped to listen when a bird sang, while the Druce swan swam as if deep in thought, studying the plants and insects of the lake's edge. And the swan that was surely Cullan saw us and paddled as fast as he could across the lake, clambering out on his webbed feet and waddling to meet us.

Wordlessly, Riona went down on one knee, and the Cullan swan laid his sleek head on her bent knee. She stroked his smooth feathers while Liam and I—and the other four swans, who had come up behind Cullan—looked away, both moved and embarrassed.

When we turned back, we could see that Riona's face was tear streaked, but her mouth was set with purpose. She stood, and the swans clustered around her, their long necks straining upward.

"There, there," she said soothingly to them. "We shall find a way to fix you. Don't worry. You will not be swans forever!" She put her palm out to the Cullan swan, and he touched it with his dark beak—a swan kiss. Then all the swans struggled back into the water, where they floated nearby, watching us with their human eyes, green and blue as my brothers' eyes had ever been.

Riona turned to me and said, "You are quite right,

Princess. These are your brothers. And I am sure it is the queen's work. I could see that she had a great power."

"I shall tell Father!" I cried, but Riona shook her head.

"That would be unwise. If she has enchanted him as well, he will never believe you. You may find yourself in danger from her if she learns that you've discovered what she has done."

I shivered. "I should not like to swim in the cold water and eat bugs," I said, watching as my brothers drifted on the lake.

"Then try to stay away from her, and heed your thoughts," Riona warned me.

"My thoughts? Can she read minds, then?" I asked uneasily, for I had thought many terrible things about Lady Orianna in the days since she had come.

"Only if you think directly at her," Liam said. I looked at him, puzzled, and he elaborated. "She cannot simply go into your mind and hear all that you are thinking. You have to address her with your thoughts, as if you were speaking to her."

"I might have done that, once or twice," I admitted. I recalled a moment, the day after she arrived, when I had not gotten out of her way quickly enough and she had stood before me and looked at me head to foot, her eyes full of criticism. I had thought, *You, Madam, should not judge me. You are not as beautiful—or as young—as you believe yourself to be,* and she had pulled back with a gasp, turned on her heel, and left me. Now I realized that she had heard that statement as clearly as if I had spoken it aloud.

Then I noticed that the sun had nearly sunk in the west, and I said, "I must get back. The queen has ordered me to appear at her ball, and I don't want her to wonder where I have been."

"No," Riona agreed. "She mustn't become suspicious. I will find out how best to break the spell, and I'll send Liam to you, for I dare not show myself at the castle again. But we must work quickly. The days are getting shorter."

"What does that matter?" I asked, confused.

"The lakes freeze, and the swans must fly south, Princess," Riona said gently. "If your brothers are not changed back by then, they will have to leave—or they will starve, or die of the cold."

"Oh!" I cried. "Then be swift, please! And come to me soon," I begged Liam, who bowed his head.

"As soon as I can, Your Highness," he replied. As he and his sister turned to go, the swans did the strange dance they had done when I first saw them, rising on the water and beating their wings furiously. In reply,

Riona waved to them, and I called out to Cullan, "Behave yourself when I am gone!" But the answering "And you too!" that I longed for did not come. My heart heavy, I sped up the long hill as Riona and Liam ran down toward town.

I was too late to appear at the queen's dinner, but already so many guests had arrived that no one seemed to notice. And the ball was unspeakably awful. Lady Orianna had chosen a dress for me to wear, one I had never seen before. She'd had it made in Ardin before she came back with Father, Mistress Tuileach told me. It had a bodice that laced so tightly that I could barely breathe, and its skirts were as heavy as lead. Ordinarily I would have loved the rich blue satin fabric, the embroidered shoes, and the lapis stones she sent me to weave on silver threads through my hair. But I shrank from it all as Mistress Tuileach tried to help me dress.

"Let me fix these in your hair," she urged me, holding out the stones as I sat before the looking glass.

"No!" I said obstinately. "The only jewel I will wear is this." I held up my sapphire necklace, its clasp broken by Cullan's strong beak.

"Oh, did it break?" Mistress Tuileach took the necklace from me. "We can string the stone on a black velvet ribbon, and it will look beautiful."

It did look beautiful. The black ribbon made my

skin seem pale and creamy, and the jewel gleamed in the hollow of my throat, making my blue-green eyes seem darker and more mysterious.

"Why does she want me at the ball?" I asked Mistress Tuileach, looking with displeasure at my image in the mirror. "Father has always said I am not old enough for balls."

"You are older than you were," Mistress Tuileach pointed out, tucking an errant curl into place. "I think the queen feels that it is time to introduce you to society."

I turned to face her, taken aback. "Do you mean that she thinks I should *marry*?" I demanded.

"You are twelve—still too young for that," Mistress Tuileach said, but her gaze slid away from mine in a way that made me very uncomfortable.

In the past, I had always watched my father's parties from a gallery above the ballroom where I could sit unobserved. I loved to see my brothers dancing, even Darrock, whose stiff, self-conscious movements made me giggle, and Druce, who usually looked as if he would rather be in the library or curled up on a window seat, reading. I had yearned to be part of the festivities for as long as I could remember. Now I would be going to the ball—but I wished I were not.

I descended the stairs to the open doors of the

ballroom with dread. I knew I looked pretty, but I did not welcome the admiring glances I received from the noblemen whom Lady Orianna had invited. I ignored them and made my way quickly over to Sir Brion, Father's old friend, who greeted me warmly.

"Princess Meriel, you are a vision of loveliness this evening!" he told me, bowing.

I dipped in a curtsy and replied, "Thank you, milord. I am glad to see a familiar face, for I think that most of these guests are the queen's. Many of them appear to have come from far away. I do not know them at all."

He nodded, looking out at the throng on the dance floor, their fine plumage of silks, satins, and jewels shimmering in the candlelight. It was a much more elegant gathering than we usually hosted; I could see no linen dresses anywhere. My brothers' friends were not there. Even the lords who were Father's usual companions were missing, except for Sir Brion.

"Aye," Sir Brion said, shaking his head sadly. "It does not seem that many of the old crowd are here. It is not the same without your brothers."

"No, not the same at all," I said in a choked voice, picturing my brothers as they swam in the waters of Heart Lake. Tears threatened, and, unable to bear Sir Brion's sympathetic gaze, I excused myself quickly.

Before I had walked more than a few feet, though, a strange gentleman bowed to me and invited me to dance. I hesitated, but he took my hand and drew me out onto the floor into a set dance, seven separate quadrilles performed with three other couples. When that set was finished, my partner handed me to another, and I danced set after set for hours as the night became a blur of movement and unfamiliar faces. Each time I tried to flee back upstairs I found myself caught in a new dance with a new partner, all handsome, all young, all strangers to me. Perhaps once I might have enjoyed the attention and the excitement, but I could not stop thinking of my brothers, and I longed to escape. By midnight I was dizzy with twirling and spinning, and quite exhausted.

At a break in the music I pulled away from my partner and fled, picking up my skirts and running out of the ballroom, down the hall, and out the side door. The queen's guards were off for the night, as guests would be coming and going until all hours, so I could move freely. The moon lighted my way as I made for the garden and found my favorite bench, sheltered inside a wooden arbor. The last roses of the season climbed up and around the trellis, and I breathed in their sweet scent as I tried to calm myself. The air was chilly with the first bite of autumn, and I thought of my brothers and the lake water, cooling.

I heard footsteps on the gravel path and groaned, then tried to make myself very inconspicuous. The last thing I wanted was to face another handsome, tedious lord. The footsteps made straight for my arbor, though, so I steeled myself and decided to be as rude as necessary to get rid of the intruder.

As the guest neared me, I said in my most scathing tone, "If you are looking for a dance partner, you will have to search elsewhere. I am weary to death of all the oafs who have stepped on my toes at the ball tonight."

There was a snort of laughter, and Riona's brother, Liam, poked his head into the arbor. "But you have not danced with me yet, Princess Meriel!" he said, grinning as he swept me a low bow. "I am known for my uncommon grace."

Before I could stop myself, I snapped, "How could one so common be uncommon in any way?" The smile slid off his face, and I clapped my hand to my mouth, but it was too late.

"Forgive my boldness, Your Highness," he said coldly. "I come with news from my sister. Here—she sends you a note." He held out a folded sheet of paper to me.

"I'm sorry," I said, but my tone was all wrong. It occurred to me that I did not really know how to apologize. To cover my embarrassment, I opened the note quickly and held it up to see it in the moonlight.

It can be done, but it is very difficult, I read. *One who loves the victims must sew them shirts from stinging nettles. When the shirts are finished and put on, the spell will be broken. But beware! If the seamstress speaks before the task is done, each word will be as a knife in the victims' hearts.*

"Oh, this is madness," I gasped, looking up at Liam. "Have you read it?"

He nodded, his expression softening a little.

"Perhaps Riona is mistaken," I suggested hopefully. How could anyone sew shirts from stinging nettles?

"She is not mistaken," he said gently. "She sent word to our mother, who is away, helping the ill. She is a full-blooded witch. This is what Mother sent back. There is no question about it."

I looked again at the paper. "Why would the queen do such a terrible thing? I do not understand."

Liam came closer, and I motioned him to sit beside me. "My mother believes that she wants her own child to be king."

"Yes," I said, low. "I have heard her say as much." I looked again at the paper. "Well, there is no one who loves them all but Father and me, and Father is under the queen's spell."

"That leaves you," Liam said, and added hard-heartedly, "I do not think you can sew five shirts from nettles, though—nor do it all in silence."

I did not blame him for his harshness, for I had insulted him. And I agreed with him. I did not think I could do it either. I could not spin nor weave, and I could sew but a little. Yet his words provoked me, and I raised fierce eyes to his and said, "I will do it. I must. Else my brothers all will die."

5

The Task:
And How It Commenced

Before Liam left the garden, we decided that I would come to the cottage as early as I could the next day, and with Riona we could make a plan for harvesting enough nettles to make the shirts. Then I went back inside, avoiding the guests who were saying their farewells to my father and the queen in the forecourt. I trudged up the stairs to my room, where Mistress Tuileach awaited me. As she helped me undress, she said, "I watched you dancing from the gallery, Princess. You were very graceful."

"Was I?" I asked distractedly. I drew my first deep

breath of the evening, glad to be uncorseted at last. "It was all so strange—I didn't know any of my partners. And the dances were all quadrilles, not the country dances that you have taught me. I couldn't tell if I danced well, or spoke well, or even looked well. It was very tiring."

"You looked very well indeed. I think some of your dance partners will be calling on you," Mistress Tuileach said as she shook out my dress. A few pieces of gravel from the garden path dropped from the hem, and she looked at me sharply.

"I truly hope they do not," I said, avoiding her gaze and climbing into bed. Then I told her, "Mistress Tuileach, I cannot come to my lessons tomorrow. There is something I must do."

"Something important?" she inquired mildly, hanging the dress in my closet.

"Very important," I said.

"Then we shall spend twice as long on lessons the next day" was her surprising response. "Your father and stepmother would like you to come to breakfast in the morning, though, and that you must do. Good night, Your Highness."

"Good night," I said. She went out of the room, and I nestled down in my pillows. I didn't think that I would sleep, but the dancing and the worry over my brothers had worn me out completely. The next moment, it seemed, my eyes opened to the sun streaming in through the window.

Mistress Tuileach helped me dress, tying my sapphire on its ribbon around my neck and braiding my hair. Then I went down to breakfast, where Father and Lady Orianna awaited me. I took scones and tea, and spooned jam onto my plate very deliberately, saying not a word and trying hard to guard my thoughts.

Finally the queen broke our silence. "Did you enjoy the ball, Meriel?" she asked.

I did not look at her. "No, not very much," I replied.

"Did you not find any partners who pleased you?"

"They were dandies. They wore too much cologne and used too much hair oil," I said, biting into a scone.

"Meriel," Father said in a scolding tone, though I could tell his heart was not in it. I turned away from them, but I could still see the queen reflected in the gold-framed mirror at the end of the table. Her eyes narrowed.

"Was there no one whom you might consider?" she persisted.

My anger overwhelmed me then. *"Consider?"* I exclaimed, turning back to look at her directly. "Do you mean consider as a husband? I am not yet thirteen! Father, do you think I am old enough to marry?"

Father looked rather blankly at me. "Why . . . no," he said. "You are still quite young." He turned to the queen. "Do you intend for her to marry, my dear?"

Lady Orianna pressed her lips together in a tight line, and I hid a smile. "Of course not, Gearalt," she said smoothly. "I was only thinking of the future. Before long, Meriel will be of an age to take a husband."

"Yes . . . before long," Father agreed. "In the meantime, though, do have some more jam, my love."

We finished breakfasting in silence, as we had begun, and then I left them together and rushed down to the cellar, where Ogan stood at guard duty.

"Your Highness," he said to me, "the queen has spoken to all of the guards about you. She noticed the other day that your dress was wet and knew you had been outside. She has made it clear that it is worth our jobs—or worse—if we let you leave."

"Oh!" I cried. "How can she do this—make me a prisoner in my own home? Will you not let me pass?"

"I cannot, Your Highness," he said regretfully.

I scowled at him. In the past, if I ordered a guard to do something, he did it without question. Now everything was different; my desires were no longer of any consequence. I spun on my heel, prepared to march away.

"I recall," Ogan said in a conversational tone, "that your brother Prince Cullan often left the castle without notice. Perhaps you know how he did it."

I turned back and stared at him. Of course I knew how Cullan did it! I grinned at Ogan, and he smiled back. As quickly and quietly as I could, I ran up to Cullan's bedchamber. It was clean and uncluttered, the bed neatly made, my brother's usual piles of clothes, hats, and boots put away. Ignoring the unnatural tidiness, I opened the long mullioned window across from the bed. Then I stood on the window seat and reached out, grabbing the thick ivy trunk that conveniently climbed up the stone wall just outside. I swung out and let myself down, hand over hand, just as I had watched Cullan do a score of times on his way to meet some girl or other in town or by the lake.

When I was clear of the castle and sure that no one observed me, I raced down the hill and onto the path that skirted the lake. As if they had been waiting for my arrival, my swan brothers swam to greet me. Quickly I went from one to the next, pressing a kiss on each bird's head.

"Darrock, Cullan, Baird, Aidan, Druce." I named them all, looking into their eyes, and told them, "Riona has found out the task I must perform to break your spell. It may take some time, but I shall do it. Only—" I paused here, looking for Cullan among the flock. His green gaze was intent on me.

"Only I cannot speak again until I am finished." Was that a glint of amusement in Cullan's eyes? I frowned at him. "If you don't think I can be silent, I will prove you wrong." The Cullan swan opened his beak and clapped it closed, the only sound a voiceless swan could make, and the others followed suit. It was as if they were applauding me, and I felt pleasure and anxiety warring within me. Perhaps I had finally begun to gain my brothers' confidence—but what if I should fail?

I left them then and ran to Riona's cottage. When I arrived, I took a moment to look more closely at it, for I had barely noticed my surroundings the previous day. It was tiny but sweet, only a little larger than a toy cottage I had once played in as a child. Autumn flowers ringed its front and spilled from window boxes, and in the cool of the morning, the chimney puffed sweet-smelling peat smoke.

I knocked, and Liam again answered the door. I was embarrassed to see him after my discourtesy the night before, and he did not look entirely pleased to see me, but he stood back to let me enter. I followed him into the cottage and stood in its main room, gazing around in fascination. Two overstuffed chairs covered with pretty floral cloth were angled toward the hearth, where a fire burned briskly. Between them was a table that held a vase overflowing with fresh fall blooms. Flowers, in fact, were everywhere—in fabrics and vases, dried and hung from the rafters in bunches, woven into the little rugs scattered here and there about the room. It was like a garden indoors. And there were birds, living birds—a thrush with one bent wing was perched on the mantel, and the crow I had seen before sat on the back of one of the chairs.

Riona came from the kitchen bearing a tray that held a teapot, three flowered cups, and a little vase of wild pansies. As she put down the tray, a small, sleek animal dashed from beneath the table, and I gave a little shriek.

"What is that?" I asked, holding up my skirts.

Liam grinned. "It's a stoat, a kind of weasel," he said. "I found it in a trap, its leg broken. I set it, it healed . . . and it stayed."

"Oh my," I said faintly. "Do your parents not mind you keeping these creatures in the house?"

"Our mother is often away. And Father . . . well, he died when we were very young. He was a sailor, and he drowned at sea."

"Ah," I said. "I'm sorry." We sat on rickety wooden chairs at the table in the main room and drank tea while Riona outlined what must be done.

"There is a field of wild stinging nettles just this side of Tiramore," she said. "The grazing animals all avoid it, and no one claims it, for it cannot be cultivated. We can collect the nettles and bring them here to spin." She pointed to a small spinning wheel in the corner.

"I don't know how to spin," I admitted.

"I will teach you," she assured me.

"But are you allowed to help?" I asked.

"Mother has said that I can help in certain ways. Liam and I can both aid in collecting the nettles, and I can show you how to spin and weave and stitch the shirts. But you must do the work yourself."

I suddenly wished that I had paid more attention to Mistress Tuileach's sewing lessons. "I am a very bad seamstress," I said glumly.

Riona and Liam exchanged a smile. "As long as the shirts hold together," Riona told me, "that will be enough."

I nodded. "And when must I stop speaking?"

"When we begin to pick," she said.

"But how can I stay mute?" I wondered. "What will I do when Father wants to speak with me, or the queen? Or my governess?"

Liam laughed, but kindly. "I can imagine that silence would be difficult for you," he said. "But I've no doubt that you will find a way." I grimaced at him, imagining the hardship of trying to avoid conversation for days, maybe weeks on end.

"You will be able to converse with us," Riona told me, and I looked at her questioningly. "You remember, we told you that the queen could hear your thoughts, if they were directed at her?"

I nodded.

"So we too can hear them, as we are half-witches. You have only to think your speech to us, and it will be as if you've spoken."

"Oh!" I said, pleased. "That will make silence much more bearable."

"For you," Liam grumbled under his breath, but his eyes told me he was teasing, and I managed to ignore him.

I put on an old dress that Riona had outgrown, for she told me that the nettles would rip and stain anything we wore. Then we started out for the field. I felt the weight of my task heavy on me as we walked, and knew I was afraid. Riona had explained that we had to soak the nettles, so that their fine, stinging needles would come off, and then dry them, even before I began to spin. It seemed an endless series of labors, and the very thought of it wearied me. My days, I saw now, had been filled with play and entertainment, and I wondered why I had complained so about the simple tasks Mistress Tuileach set me. I did not know how to work. How could I possibly pick and soak and dry, spin and weave and sew, and do it all before the lake froze?

To distract myself—and with the prospect of a long silence looming before me—I began to talk, almost desperately. I chattered to Riona and Liam about balls and parties and dinners in the palace, about my brothers' various adventures, about hunting and jousts, gowns and horses. I could tell that Riona enjoyed the bits that featured Cullan, and Liam seemed to like hearing about the hunts and swordplay. By the time we reached the field, I was tired of my own voice, but I had one last thing to say. I turned to Liam.

"I am so very sorry for calling you common last night," I told him, the words that I had rehearsed spilling from me almost too fast to be understood. My voice cracked on the word *common*. "It was terribly impolite, and I didn't mean it. I truly hope that you will forgive me." This was the most—or perhaps the only—heartfelt apology I had ever made, and I waited anxiously to hear Liam's reply.

His eyes crinkled in a smile, and he bowed his head to me. "You were vexed and tired," he said graciously.

"Of course I forgive you."

I sighed with relief. It had not gone as badly as I had feared at all.

"And," he went on, "it is not the first time you were rude to me."

"Liam!" Riona said, shocked.

"No, go on," I said. "What did I do?"

"It was a year ago, or more," Liam told me. "You had a bird in a cage, and it was ailing. It would not eat."

I recalled it well. It was a lark, and it had stopped singing its sweet song and would only sit on a silver perch and stare out my window.

"Yes," I said in a low voice. "I remember."

"I let it go," he reminded me. "I opened the cage and the window, and it flew to freedom, and you said—"

"Oh, don't!" I interrupted him. "I am dreadful, I know. I'm sorry. Please, forgive me!"

He grinned at me and said, "It is all in the past. I just wanted to be sure you remembered we had met before."

"I do remember now," I said, ashamed. "You were right; a lark should not be caged. I have not had a bird since."

"Liam, stop tormenting her," Riona scolded her brother. "We must begin our picking."

"You are both very kind to help me," I said awkwardly,

for I was no more practiced at gratitude than apology. "Collecting the nettles will surely hurt you—you don't have to do it."

"Of course we must," Riona replied gently, and I remembered how lovingly and sadly she had stroked Cullan's feathered wings.

"We're glad to help you," Liam added, placing a warm hand over mine. I looked at his face, realizing all at once that he was as handsome, with his bright blue eyes and dark curls, as his sister was pretty. The thought made me flush, and I pulled my hand away.

"We should start," I said abruptly, and we turned to the field.

"These are nettles," Riona told me, pointing to a weedy plant with a thick stem and jagged leaves that grew in profusion in the barren-looking soil. "The stings come from the stem, and the needles are very thin and hard to see. It's impossible to avoid them. I've brought gloves—they will help to protect your hands."

I took the thick gloves she held out to me, wrinkling my nose at their appearance. They looked rough and peasantlike and were too big for me, so when I grasped the first nettle by its tough stem and pulled, one of the gloves slid down, leaving my wrist exposed. The nettle brushed against it, and my breath hissed out between my teeth as I held back a cry. I had never been stung by a nettle before. It was like a dozen stab-bing pinpricks that grew in intensity until I was sure I would wail aloud. I held my breath, thinking of what would happen if I spoke: *each word will be as a knife in the vic-tims' hearts.* Then suddenly the pain faded, and I was left with a sore, reddened patch on my wrist that itched and burned.

I pulled up the glove and yanked hard near the base of the plant, jerking the nettle out of the ground by the roots. Then I went on to the next. Behind me, Riona and Liam began to gather the plants into bundles. I endured sting after sting as my gloves slid down or I made the mistake of wiping my neck or brow with a gloved hand, for the stinging needles clung to the gloves. During the first hour I wept as I worked, but then I grew more accustomed to the pain. I set my jaw and trudged silently onward through the field.

When the sun began to lower in the sky, Riona said that we must stop. My arms and shoulders ached, and I was exhausted. We carried the bundles back to the cot-tage and into the garden, where an enormous kettle of water waited. I placed the nettles in the water to soak, as Riona instructed. Then I stripped off the gloves, winc-ing at the raw patches on my wrists and hands where the gloves had slipped as I picked.

"I have something to soothe the stings," Riona said,

leading me inside. She settled me by the fire, dislodging a small rabbit that nestled in the chair, and brought a bowl of a lavender-scented cream from the kitchen. Kneeling beside me, she smoothed the cream onto my hands and arms, my neck and face where the skin burned and itched. Immediately I felt better.

"This is made from dock leaves from my garden," Riona told me, "mashed into a paste and mixed with lavender. The lavender is just for the scent." I nodded weakly at her and sighed. *What must I do next?* I thought.

As if I had spoken aloud, Riona said, "The soaked nettles must be dried tomorrow, and you will have to pick many more. What you have gathered will make only a single shirt."

I stared at her, amazed that she had actually heard my thoughts. A moment, later, though, I was horrified. I had thought I'd picked enough for all the shirts. *No, that cannot be!* I thought. *I can't do this for four more days!*

"Of course you can, Princess," she said gently, finishing with the unguent and standing up. "Now, I think we have all earned a good tea. Then you must change and get back."

We had tea, and I practiced my new mode of communication. It took some concentration, for I was used to speaking without thinking overmuch about what I said.

The tea is delicious, I thought at Riona.

"It is a restorative, made from cowslip flowers and red clover," she replied. "That was very nice and clear, Your Highness!"

You must both call me Meriel, I thought at them, wondering if two could hear me at once. They looked surprised.

"No," protested Liam, "that doesn't seem . . . right."

I smiled at him. *You are doing so much for me and for my brothers,* I told them. *It would not be right if you were to call me anything else.* They smiled back at me then, and my heart was lighter as I changed into my own dress and started back toward the castle.

I stopped at the lake, eerie in the gathering dusk. Mist was rising from its cold water, and my snow-white swan brothers swam through the vapor like ghosts. They gathered around me eagerly, but I, of course, could tell them nothing. I shook my head and pointed to my closed mouth, reminding them of my silence, but still they seemed uneasy. I did not want to leave them there, though it was some small comfort to me that I was working to help them.

I hurried home as darkness descended, climbing back up the vine to get to Cullan's window. I found this much more difficult than climbing down, especially with my poor blistered palms. But I managed, and then had to spend an uncomfortable evening dining with Father, Lady Orianna, and several guests. I tried to keep my wounded hands and arms out of sight and my aching back straight in my chair. Luckily, the conversation flowed without stopping at me, so my silence was not noted. I nodded and smiled when necessary and nearly fell asleep over my gooseberry tart. When the gathering broke up, I staggered to my room. Mistress Tuileach had already gone to bed, so I lay down on my coverlet without disrobing and was asleep in an instant.

In the morning I met Mistress Tuileach in the salon, for I knew I could not miss my lessons again. I was fearful that my silence would betray me and had not worked out a convincing way to avoid speaking. I poured tea neatly, smiling and nodding, and played a piece at the pianoforte in the music room. To my great relief, my governess did not ask me to sing or to practice my French. She dismissed me before noon, saying, "You must be sure not to strain your throat, child, if you are feeling a cold coming on." I looked at her sharply, but she only gave me her customary brisk nod, and I touched my throat delicately and nodded back.

I clambered out Cullan's window and down the thick vine; then, making sure I was not observed, I sped to Riona's cottage. The afternoon passed in much the same way as the day before, as I picked and soaked nettles, laid them to dry in the garden, and picked and soaked more.

We had a series of clear, crisp days, and I followed the same schedule, with silent lessons in the morning, work in the afternoon, and a silent dinner with Father, Lady Orianna, and whatever guests or councilors they were entertaining each evening. The queen had constant visitors, lords and ladies from Ardin whom she had known before she met Father, and I was grateful that her attention was taken up with them. It gave her less time to notice me. And Father—well, he was utterly captivated by his new wife. Though it pained me to see that he did not note my silence or my damaged hands, I was thankful for his distraction as well.

By the fourth day of picking I felt stronger and less exhausted from the work. I did not grow used to the nettles' sting, though, and each afternoon's labor began with pain and tears. But I would think of Baird's face as he sang or Aidan's joyful whoop as he leaped a stile on his horse, and my memories gave me the strength to go on. At last, as the fifth afternoon waned, Riona said I had collected enough nettles, and I began to spin, sitting at the wheel in the corner of the cottage's main room.

The spinning was not difficult, but the nettle fibers had to pass between my fingers as I spun them into thread, so I developed blisters that quickly became thick calluses. Red and raw, my hands were no longer those of a princess. Not even a merchant or a good-wife would have hands like mine; they were a laborer's hands. I mourned them at first, but I was proud, too, of the work that had torn and hardened them and made them ugly.

As I spun, Liam told me stories—old tales of heroes and battles—which were exciting enough to help pass the time. He especially liked the tales of the Fianna, men who had to pass terrible tests to join their warrior groups. With their long hair braided, they had to run through the forest, pursued by the other Fianna. If they were captured, or if their braids caught on a bough, or if a branch cracked under their feet, they would fail the test—and they had to recite poetry as they ran.

Poet warriors! I marveled. *What a strange and wonderful breed of men they must have been.*

"That was in the days when all the folk of Faerie—fairies, elves, monsters, witches good and bad—lived among people. It was not such a good time, though it makes for good tales," Riona said. "Many of the Faerie folk are cruel and don't care at all about what their deeds do to humans. Now only the witches live with people, for they—we—are closer to humankind than any of the others. Some have married humans, as Mother did, and there are many of us who are half witch. As for the rest of the Faerie folk, it is better that they stay below ground in their own land."

"There are rumors, though . . . ," Liam mused.

Rumors of what?

"Well, people say that the creatures of Faerie are stirring again—that some are making their way back up to us."

Why should they do that? I asked. *Do they not like it in their own land?*

"That is their home, but they do not like being forced to stay there," Riona replied. "They are kept below by powerful spells that witches like our mother have cast to protect us. Always some have managed to escape, but now it seems that more and more are coming up. We fear that they want to be part of both worlds—or even to rule both worlds, their own and ours."

I thought of the legends surrounding Heart Lake, but said nothing.

When I grew weary of Liam's tales of swordfights and sieges, he described his own plans for the future. He wanted to study physic, the medical art, but to apply the healing skills he learned to animals rather than humans.

"Mother travels from village to village as a healer," he explained. "But my skills seem to work best on animals. That rabbit, now"—he pointed to the rabbit that sat beside Riona as she crushed herbs with a mortar and pestle—"she had been shot by someone's arrow and left to die. I did not think she would survive, but with Riona's herbs, she's done very well."

"It's your touch, Brother, as much as my plants," Riona said fondly. "The animals seem to know he won't hurt them. They do not mind when he works on them, and many of them stay on with us." She stroked the rabbit's fine fur, and its long ears twitched with pleasure. "And though a stoat and a rabbit are mortal enemies in the wild, here they have grown up together and are friends." It was true; I had seen the stoat and rabbit sleeping together in a basket by the fire, curled around each other.

Liam and Riona taught me the medicinal properties of the herbs in their garden: yarrow, to treat headaches; coriander, which reduced fever; rosemary, to heal disease and help memory; fennel, to stop colic in a fussy baby. Every plant, it seemed, had a use, and I was fascinated to learn them. In fact, I was fascinated by nearly everything Liam and Riona did and said. I was unaccustomed to being with others near my own age, except for my brothers, for there were no other princesses living near Castle Rua, and few noble children. I had spent all my time vying for my brothers' attention and affection. Now I began to realize that there had been a great lack in my life, and despite the wearisome nature of my task, I cherished the hours I spent at the little cottage.

One afternoon, when I had been spinning for three or four days, I was able to see brother and sister do their work. A knock sounded at the door, and Riona opened it to find a box there, holding an injured squirrel. She carried it inside after looking about for the person who had left it, but there was no one in sight.

"They often come to us thus," she sighed, lifting out the little animal with its long, bushy tail. "Some of the children are frightened of witches and run off, for it is not always clear if we are good or bad." The squirrel wriggled and squeaked, but when Liam took it from her it settled in his hands and lay there quietly, its eyes bright and suspicious.

"Its paw is crushed," he said, looking the squirrel over carefully. "Perhaps it was caught between rocks as it tried to escape some terrible danger."

He laid it gently in a box lined with soft grasses, and the rabbit and stoat came to sniff at it, backing away when it chittered wildly at them. Liam and Riona mixed herbs together and made a paste, which Liam applied to the wounded paw. The squirrel tried to lick it off and made a face of such dismay at the taste that I had to cover my mouth to keep the laughter in. Each afternoon when I arrived I checked on it, and in a matter of days the paw was healed. The squirrel did not stay on with the other animals but ran back to the small stand of woods not far from the cottage, where it could forage for nuts. Often we could hear it chittering to us from a nearby tree.

It took over a week to spin the nettles, but when at last I was finished, I had great spindles of coarse thread that I now needed to weave into cloth. Riona brought out her hand loom, which was small enough to carry, and instructed me on how to use it. Immediately I thought, *Oh, can I weave at the lake, and see my brothers?*

Riona pursed her lips. "Is it safe?" she wondered. "Have you ever seen guards there?"

I shook my head. *No, never,* I replied, for I passed the lake each day as I went to and fro. *The queen keeps them at the castle—to confine me!* I smiled, thinking of my daily escape.

"Then I think it is a fine idea," Riona said. "The day will be warm tomorrow—it should be lovely there."

I was very skilled at sneaking from the castle by this time. As soon as my lessons were finished the next day, I dashed down to the lake, eager to spend time with my brothers. Liam and Riona had not yet arrived with my loom and thread, so I could not begin working. I could see the swans across the water, dabbling in the weeds for food, but they did not notice me as I waved. I started to walk around the wide shoreline to them, but then I thought that if I went the other way—to the narrow end of the lake and around—it would be a shorter distance. I knew, too, that the narrow point was rumored to be the source of the Faerie spring, and I was drawn to see what was there. I did not quite believe in the lands and creatures Riona and Liam had described to me. Besides, the day was fine, the sun bright—what ill could befall me?

I had not gone far before I began to regret my impulse. There was no real path; the way was thick with thorny bushes that grabbed and tore my skirts. The mist that always hung over this part of the lake even on fine days thickened around me, and I grew confused. It seemed that I had been walking much longer than I should have to reach the lake's end. I tried to keep the water in sight on my right-hand side, but the shore was rocky, and I had to move away from it. I was about to give up and start back when I heard a strange, sweet sound. It was like water gently plashing from a fountain, and like the thrum of a harp at the same time. It seemed to call me forward.

I emerged from the damp mist into a clearing at the foot of the lake, the sharp V of its heart shape. At the very point of the V, a spring bubbled gently out from the rocks, and I moved closer to it. Where the spring rose up from the earth, there was a cavelike opening, a gap in the ground that seemed, at first sight, perfectly dark. When I looked again, though, I believed that I could see a welcoming radiance deep within it and hear the faint sound of lute and bells. The light and music pulled at me, and again I moved toward the chasm. I could almost make out voices in the song—or was it just the sound of water moving over rocks? The uncanny light issued forth, and with it came a wondrous fragrance: the scent of every delicious thing I had ever tasted and every beautiful flower I had ever smelled. I breathed in roses and lilacs, spun sugar and honey cakes and raspberries, until I was dizzy and breathless.

And now the voices were even clearer. They sang my name and spoke to me: "Princess Meriel!" they murmured. "Come to us! Bide with us! We will dress you in silks and velvets; we will seat you on a golden throne. You will be loved and honored, and your brothers will return to you again. O Princess, come to us! Bide with us!"

I looked into the springwater at my feet, and there I could see an empty golden throne. I knelt to view the scene more closely. Behind the throne were the forms of lovely women and handsome men, and I saw my brothers among them, restored to their human shapes, beckoning to me. How strong and handsome they looked! The vision was as clear as a painting. I knew that if only I could find my way into it, my hands would become white and smooth again, and I would be beautiful and beloved and completely happy. My face dipped lower toward the water, and the words *Yes, yes, I am coming!* tried to force themselves past my lips. I was utterly lost.

The Governess:
And What She Knew

Suddenly there came a violent yank on the back of my cloak, and I tumbled over onto my backside, a sharp rock digging into my leg. It was like awakening from the most wonderful dream—or was it the most frightful nightmare?

"Meriel!" I heard Liam cry, in a voice that was equal parts worry and anger. "What are you doing? Get away from there!"

I scrabbled backward, away from the chasm and the enchanted spring. I was light-headed and bewildered, and I could not seem to make my legs work properly.

Liam hauled me to my feet as I shook my head, trying to throw off the spell I had been under.

"That is the way to Faerie," he admonished me, "and it is not for mortals. Did you think you could just stop by for a visit?"

I—I do not know what I was thinking, I told him as my senses returned to me. *I saw . . . something marvelous. There was a throne . . . there were people singing. . . .*

"Those were not people, and if you had gone, you would never have returned," Liam said flatly, pulling me away. "The legends of this place are true—why do you think no one fishes or swims here? The spring leads to the lands below, and the rumors are right. The door is opening wide. If you go down, there is no escape."

I looked at the spring, and the deep, dark gash in the earth, and I shuddered. *I wanted to go . . . ,* I said weakly.

"They tell you what you want to hear and show you what you long to see," Liam said, helping me over the rocks as we started back. "They promise you what you want most in the world."

My brothers . . .

"But it is all a lie," he told me fiercely. "You must never come here alone again, do you hear?"

I nodded meekly. Now that I was away from the spring, the memory of what I had seen and heard and smelled no longer seemed wonderful, but terrible. I couldn't imagine what my fate would have been had Liam not pulled me back.

We joined Riona on the shore at the wide end of the lake, far from the menacing spring. Liam told her what had happened, and she looked horrified.

"The spring is one of the gateways to Faerie, Meriel. Did you not believe the stories?" she asked me, and I shook my head. "They are all true, and there are tales no one has ever told as well, for those unfortunate ones never came back. Had you never heard—" She broke off, perhaps not wanting to frighten me.

No, go on, I urged her. I wanted to know what I had escaped, to lessen the pull of the lovely vision I had seen.

"Many, many years ago, there was a man named Fergus—a blacksmith, I think he was. As the story goes, he was fishing in the lake, as no one dares today, and went around to the far side, for he did not believe in the Faerie spring. He called to Faerie and challenged its inhabitants to appear. And up from the depths came a muirdris." Her voice dropped to a whisper.

A muirdris? I asked uneasily.

"A monster so unbearably dreadful to look upon that to set eyes on it may kill the viewer. When Fergus saw it, his face froze in a grotesque mirror of the monster's, and it stayed that way for the rest of his life."

"He lived in seclusion, they say, until he died," Liam told me. "He dared not be seen by anyone, for fear that the horror of his own face would transform others as the muirdris had done to him."

I shivered, looking toward the narrow end of the lake and trying to imagine a creature so frightful that it could freeze men's faces.

"There are many beasts that terrible who live in the lands below," Riona said. Then she patted my arm. "We are safe here, I think, but do not go near the spring again!"

The lake sparkled innocently in the October sunlight, and leaves floated on its surface. I noticed that the flocks of ducks and geese seemed smaller. Some had surely flown south already, and the thought troubled me. Soon frost would rime the meadow grasses, and the lake would begin to freeze. What would my brothers do then?

The swans came and settled among us. Riona warned them of the spring and told them what I had seen. Darrock clacked his beak reprovingly at me. Druce flapped his wings wildly, as if to say "Beware!" and I recalled that he had read books about the Faerie folk and knew much about them. My brothers all seemed to understand that they must stay away from the far end of the lake.

They watched curiously as Riona and I set up the loom, and she told them what I was doing and why. I began to weave with her help, first looping warp threads from the top crosspiece of the loom to the bottom and back again. Then I passed the weft threads through the warp threads and pushed them down, making a row of woven fabric. Over and over I did this. It was not difficult or painful, like picking the nettles, only repetitive and tedious. As I wove, Cullan laid his sleek white head in Riona's lap, and she began to sing in a clear, high voice.

> "'We watch the swans that sleep in a shadowy place,
> And now and again one wakes and uplifts its head;
> How still you are—your gaze is on my face—
> We watch the swans and never a word is said.'"

The Baird swan was entranced, his slender neck swaying to the rhythm of the tune, but the song was too sad for me, and tears came to my eyes. Seeing my distress, Liam leaped up and devised a game where he threw a small stone and the swans vied to catch it in their black beaks. Even in swan form, Aidan excelled at the sport. The sounds of Liam and Riona laughing and the swans clapping beaks gladdened me as I worked, making the time pass quickly, and I was astonished to see a brownish-colored fabric begin to emerge from the threads under my fingers. I interrupted the game, motioning Liam over to look.

"That's very good, Meriel," he said kindly.

It's cloth! I exclaimed silently, annoyed that he did not appreciate it more.

"Indeed it is," he replied, suppressing a smile. It was little enough to him, but I had never made anything before, and to me it seemed almost magical. I worked intently until dusk and returned to the castle satisfied with what I had accomplished.

Several days passed in this way. My brothers had now been in their swan guise for nearly three weeks. I had thus far managed to keep my distance from the queen, though one night at dinner I caught her looking at me, a strange expression on her face. Feeling more and more anxious, I sped up my work.

The next morning I woke to rain and had to weave at the cottage. After that the weather changed. We wrapped blankets around us as we sat by the lake. My fingers grew stiff with the cold, and I had to stop now and then to warm them. When the wind blew, I thought longingly of the cozy hearth fire in the cottage, but I did not want to leave the lakeside. I was glad to be able to keep an eye on my brothers.

I noticed, on a cold gray afternoon, that one of the

swans seemed listless, a little dazed. I had spent enough time watching my brothers to know that it was Aidan who was ailing. He did not poke among the water plants for food, but floated sluggishly in the shallows.

Liam, I said uneasily, *is something wrong with Aidan?*

Liam looked across the water and grew troubled. "He doesn't seem well," he noted. He called the swans over, but Aidan did not come. Wincing at the chill of the lake, Liam waded out to him. He stroked the swan's long neck gently and looked him over closely, then splashed back. I turned worried eyes to him when he told me, "Aidan may be ill, but I hope that he is simply tired and cold. Swans do not do well when the weather turns. I'll see what we have at home that may help him."

I wove on anxiously, awaiting Liam's return. Finally he came back bearing a small vessel with a tincture inside. "Black walnut, wormwood, goldenrod, and thyme. That will increase his energy and drive away any pests that may be bothering him." When Riona nodded her approval, Liam waded out again and, with a dropper, fed the mixture to Aidan. By the next day he seemed livelier, and Liam gave him another dropperful and dosed the others, to prevent the same lethargy from striking them.

Thank you, I said to him with gratitude. *You have a true skill.*

He smiled at me. "Do you know what a group of swans is called?" he asked.

I shook my head.

"A group of most birds is a flock, but a gathering of swans is also called a lamentation. It's strange, because ordinarily they don't seem like sad birds."

It is perfect for this group, though, I said forlornly, gazing at my brothers as they swam. *A lamentation of swans.*

The nights were bitter now, and I saw the water plants begin to wither. Each day I wove a little faster, until I was very nearly done weaving all the thread to cloth. Then one evening, I was called to dine with Father and the queen, for they were leaving in the morning to visit dignitaries in Coilin. Father had spoken of bringing me along; he did not like to leave me alone in the castle with my brothers gone, but Lady Orianna had convinced him that I would be safe enough with the guards and councilors and my governess for protection. I was greatly relieved.

For the past several nights, I had eaten my dinner silently in my room with Mistress Tuileach. She did not press me to speak or say anything about my poor hands, and I wondered, not for the first time, why she had not asked me to explain where I went each day or what I did. I surmised that she must have told Father I was unwell, or I would not have been permitted to eat alone. But this night, there would be no reprieve.

"You must wear this gown," Mistress Tuileach advised me, laying out an overdress with long sleeves that ended in points over my hands, covering them most cleverly. I smiled at her gratefully and slipped on the dress. We went downstairs, and at the door to the dining hall she grasped my shoulders.

"I will be just outside the door," she said in a low voice. The concern in her eyes made me feel even more anxious myself. It was clear that Mistress Tuileach did not like the queen and avoided her at any cost. I had seen them in the same room only once, briefly, in Lady Orianna's first week with us, and Mistress Tuileach had kept her head down and had spoken not a word. I wondered suddenly whether perhaps my governess feared the queen.

The long table was laid for only three, with my father at the head and Lady Orianna, sumptuous in midnight-blue velvet, at his right. My place was opposite hers. My heart began to beat faster.

The soup course did not go badly. Father spoke of his day—his meetings with advisors, his audiences with his subjects.

"I cannot think why you allow those people in," the queen complained. "They are only peasants. Their lives are good enough under your benevolent rule. What right do they have to complain?"

"It is tradition, my dear," Father said mildly. "I have always held audiences on Wednesdays. As their over-lord, I am responsible for their well-being. If they are not living well or happily, and I can help them, should I not do it?" He sounded a little like my father of old, but there was no strength behind his words, and his eyes were always on the queen.

"I do not think the audiences are necessary," she told him. "I believe you should stop them."

"Stop them?" Father said. His expression was con-fused, but then he smiled, like a child. "Why yes, my dear, if that is what you wish." I stared at the cloth covering the table, trying to keep my mind quiet, my thoughts calm.

Lady Orianna dabbed delicately at her mouth with a linen napkin as servants removed the bowls and brought in plates of fowl. I tried not to breathe in the smell of them, for I had found in the last fortnight that I could no longer eat poultry of any kind. Even a chicken, roasted and laid on a platter, was a grim reminder of my swan brothers.

"You are far too kind to your subjects, Gearalt," the queen said. "Your indulgence is one of your greatest weaknesses." Father looked hurt, and she quickly added, "But your generous heart was one of my foremost reasons for marrying you. I would have you no other way."

Father laughed and replied, "That is good, for you will get me no other way!" But I noted how the queen smiled to herself at his words.

Then her gaze fell on me, and I lowered my eyes, wishing I were invisible.

"And you, Meriel," she said in a deceptively pleasant voice, "how have you spent the day? Your governess has told your father that you were ailing. Are you quite well now? Your appetite does not seem hearty."

I bought myself time by sipping from my goblet, then cleared my throat, forcing a cough that I hoped sounded authentic.

"Speak up, child!" she urged me. "Your father was quite anxious about your health, but I kept him from you so he would not sicken himself. Are you fully recovered?"

The idea that she had refused to let Father see me enraged me, but I held in my anger and pointed to my throat, trying to convince her that it was sore enough to prevent speaking. But to my dismay, the movement pulled back my sleeve, exposing a callused hand.

Lady Orianna's eyes narrowed at the sight, and

Father looked shocked.

"Meriel, what have you been doing with your hands?" he asked. "Show them to us!"

Slowly, with fear building in me, I laid my hands on the table, staring down at them. Against the white cloth they looked terrible, chapped and red and rough.

"She has been working as a washerwoman!" exclaimed Lady Orianna. "Or hoeing and scything in the fields!"

"Is this true, Meriel?" Father asked, bewildered.

I shook my head, trembling.

"Why do you not speak, child?" Lady Orianna asked me. I tried as hard as I could to keep my mind a blank, afraid that she would hear the thoughts that raced through me. The more I tried to suppress them, though, the louder they seemed to chorus in my head. I dared not look at her, but when I lifted my gaze from the table I saw her reflected in the mirror she had hung at the end of the room. Our eyes met in the mirror, and I could see a sudden awareness dawning in her expression.

I rose abruptly, rocking the table. As I stood, my goblet crashed to the floor, shattering into a hundred tiny pieces. At the sound, the door to the hall flew open. Mistress Tuileach stood there, and I ran to her.

Help me! I thought in desperation.

"I shall," she replied quietly. My mouth dropped open in astonishment as she said to my father and the queen, "The princess is ill, and she must go straight to bed. Please excuse us, Your Majesties." And with that, she put an arm around me and pulled me from the room.

7

The Spring:
And What It Held

Back in my bedchamber I quickly put on my nightdress and climbed into bed, for Mistress Tuileach feared that my father, in his concern, would follow us.

You are a witch? I asked her silently as I settled myself. I had half suspected, wondering for weeks why she had not pressed me to speak, why she avoided the queen, why she watched me so closely yet said so little.

"On my mother's side only," she told me, plumping up my pillows. "There are more of us half-witches about than you would guess! Now, tell me, at once. I

have been studying you this past month, and I have fig-
ured some things out, but I do not know all."

I described the queen's wicked enchantment and the
cure, and she nodded, unsurprised. Then I told her of
Riona and Liam and what I had accomplished so far in
my task—the picking of the nettles, the spinning, the
weaving.

"So you have yet to stitch the shirts?" she asked, and
I nodded. Her lips curled in a wry smile, and I knew
she was thinking of the many ways I had found to avoid
learning to sew.

You knew best, I admitted, shamefaced.

"Keep that in mind, Princess!" she admonished me,
but her tone was fond. Then there was a knock at the
door. I slipped down among my pillows and closed my
eyes.

Mistress Tuileach let Father in, and he hurried to
my bedside.

"She is asleep," Mistress Tuileach whispered. "I
think it was just a small relapse, brought on by worry
and lack of rest. She has been missing her brothers
dreadfully and has had many wakeful nights."

"I should not go away," Father said in a low voice.
"What if she were to worsen? Or perhaps the queen
could stay behind to care for her."

Mistress Tuileach drew in a sharp breath at that

idea. "I think that is unnecessary, Your Majesty," she said. "The princess is much better and will continue to improve, I am sure. And if anything were to happen, a swift rider could reach you within hours."

"True," Father mused. "If it were not such an important meeting . . . she is very precious to me, you know." His words warmed my heart. "Will you watch her carefully, and send for me if there is any change?"

"I will, Your Majesty," Mistress Tuileach assured him.

"And what of her hands?" Father asked. "Do you know what she has been doing?"

Mistress Tuileach spoke smoothly. "It was to be a surprise, Your Majesty. She has developed a great interest in healing herbs, and was readying a plot for an herb garden to be planted in the spring. I think she has worked too hard at it, for she has harmed her hands and weakened her health. I should have kept a closer watch on her." I was amazed at her cleverness—and at the fact that she had learned my new interest, though of course I had not said a word about it.

"Oh!" Father said. "Healing herbs—is that a suitable pastime for a princess?"

"I believe that it is," Mistress Tuileach replied. "Many's the queen who has used her skill at herbology to aid her subjects. That is why I have encouraged it."

"Very well," Father said. "But I think you should

keep her from that task while we are away. I do not want her to overwork herself again. And do something about her hands. They are a terrible sight!"

"I will, Your Majesty," Mistress Tuileach promised again. I felt Father press a kiss on my brow and then heard him go out. When the door clicked behind him, I opened my eyes.

That was quick thinking! I said silently, with great admiration.

"You see that I am good for something besides tedious lessons and endless nagging," Mistress Tuileach replied. I realized she was using words that I had thought at her many times over the years, and I blushed. For the second time in my life, I apologized and meant it.

Forgive me, I thought. *You have been very good to me.*

She smiled then, and I saw how it transformed her long face, making it almost pretty. I was beginning to understand that her face was very dear to me.

"You must try to sleep, child," she advised me. "Rest while you can. The queen is highly suspicious of us both. By keeping my distance, I have been able to prevent her from hearing my thoughts since she arrived, but she is very strong. Once she sets her mind to it, I shall be exposed. We must get much done while she is away. We have very little time."

We! I now had another ally. *Surely three half-witches—you, Riona, and Liam—can outwit a single full-blooded witch,* I said, encouraged. But my governess shook her head.

"The lady Orianna is very powerful. She wants your father, and a child, and the kingdom for herself. She has done her best to make that happen. And I fear that she has a purpose even darker than that, though I have not been able to discover it yet. Whatever it may be, only you stand in her way now."

Instead of frightening me, Mistress Tuileach's words made me all the more resolute. I would weave until my hands bled, and sew with lightning speed—all day and all night if I must!

I rose before dawn and with Mistress Tuileach's help readied myself to go down to the lake, where I would meet Riona and Liam for the day's weaving. I was determined to finish the cloth that day and begin sewing the shirts. Father and Lady Orianna left at daybreak, and soon after I climbed down the ivy and slipped away from the castle, taking care that the guards were inside and could not see me.

Riona and Liam were already waiting for me on the shore when I arrived. As I worked I silently told Riona and Liam of the scene at dinner and my governess's surprising revelation, and Riona repeated my tale to the swans. They waved their necks back and forth as they listened to the description of Lady Orianna's behavior and clapped their beaks approvingly when they heard of Mistress Tuileach's unveiling as a half-witch.

I worked through the day with great will and concentration. Liam and Riona told stories and sang to keep me company, but eventually they drifted off into sleep. By the time the shadows grew long, I had finally finished making my cloth. I decided to take it back to the castle, where I could cut it and pin it into shirt shapes to be stitched. But as I rose, stretching the stiffness from my legs, I noticed that the swans were no longer near us. I shook Liam, waking him.

Where are my brothers? I demanded silently. He stood and yawned and looked around, growing more alert as he realized he could not see them on the water.

"Riona!" he called sharply, for she was napping too. "The swans are gone!"

We looked across the lake, where the geese and ducks still swam, but saw no sign of them.

They would not have flown south, would they? I asked anxiously.

"No, no, there is still food for them, and the lake is unfrozen," Riona assured me. "I am afraid, though, that they may have paddled to the far end." We looked at one another, and I knew my eyes were wide with worry. I did not want to go back to the Faerie spring.

"We must look for them," Liam said decisively. "We will be safe if we stay together." I nodded, and we set out for the narrow part of the lake. Again the brambles tore my clothes, and my fine shoes were quickly ruined, but I didn't care. A great unease was growing in me.

As we approached the lake's end, tendrils of cold, damp fog began to curl around us. They were almost like arms, or the tentacles of nameless beasts. I could feel their weight on my shoulders, clutching around my waist and about my ankles. Shivering, I reached out to Liam, and he took my hand. His touch made me feel a little braver. But there was still no sign of my brothers. Indeed, the mist was so thick now that we could see only a few feet in any direction. Still, we stumbled on.

All at once the air cleared completely, and I gasped. There, in front of me, was the spring, bubbling up among mossy rocks just as it had when I saw it before. My brothers were swimming at the place where the spring ran into the lake. Perched on a rock above them was a woman in a long silvery dress.

She was heartbreakingly beautiful, and she was not human. Her face was a woman's, though far lovelier than any I had ever seen, even Lady Orianna's. But her waist-length hair, which she combed as we watched, was as green as the moss on her rock, and the hands that grasped her comb were webbed.

"It is a merrow!" Riona whispered.

I clutched Liam's hand more tightly. There were many tales of merrows—mermaid-like creatures that could take human form. Sometimes, I had heard, they were friendly, but more often their actions were malevolent. When this merrow fastened her gaze on me, I could see at once that she was of the second kind.

As the swans stretched their long necks toward her, the merrow opened her mouth and began to sing. Her voice was exquisite, as pure as the springwater that flowed beneath her. At first I could not understand her song; it seemed to be in another language. But as I strained to listen, the words grew clearer and clearer, and I shuddered at what they might mean.

> "'The trees are in their autumn beauty,
> The woodland paths are dry,
> Under the October twilight the water
> Mirrors a still sky;
> Upon the brimming water among the stones
> Are five once-human swans.

> "'And now they drift on the still water,
> Mysterious, beautiful;
> Among what rushes will they build,
> By what lake's edge or pool

Delight men's eyes, when you awake some day
To find they have flown away?'"

The merrow's song, with its hint that the swans would soon be gone, terrified me, and I longed to confront her, to shout at her, to demand that she leave my brothers alone. *What does she want?* I asked Liam.

He pointed to the swans. They pressed toward the merrow, two of them appearing especially entranced by her song. One I presumed was Baird, by the way his head swayed to the tune. The other, clearly, was Cullan.

I turned to see Riona's reaction. Her face was like a sky on a stormy day: first a cloud of dismay, then a flash of alarm, then finally a thunderhead of anger passed over it. I grabbed at her skirt as she pushed past me toward the merrow.

Wait! I cautioned her. *Is the creature not dangerous?*

"I have my own small magic," Riona declared. "She shall not take them—not if I can stop it!"

The merrow, her song finished, turned luminous gray-green eyes to us. "They want to go with me, Lady," she said in a voice like water over stone. "They must do as they wish."

"They are enchanted!" Riona cried. "They want what their enchantress wants—it is not their own desire."

"And I too want what their enchantress wants,"

said the merrow. I felt a stab of fear. So this was Lady Orianna's doing!

"Meriel," Liam whispered, "look about you. Try to find a cap made of feathers—a calotte. It must be near to her. It is our only chance. Riona is not strong enough to keep her from taking your brothers."

But what—, I began. A cap? Was there a cap in the stories I had heard?

"She cannot swim back to Faerie without the cap," he said. "Hurry!"

I saw that the merrow had begun to move slowly backward, toward the chasm in the earth that had called to me before. I forced my eyes from her and, with Liam, began to search among the rocks and brambles. As we hunted, we heard Riona muttering strings of words in a low tone. After each pronouncement, I looked up and saw the merrow's backward progression briefly halted. The swans in front of her stopped as well, their webbed feet pushing frantically against the force of the spring that flowed into the lake. But moment by moment, the merrow shook off Riona's spell and resumed her slow movement toward the opening to Faerie, pulling the swans along with her.

I saw no sign of a cap, but Liam suddenly said, "It must be behind her!" He leaped past the merrow. She turned as quickly as she could, but Riona's chanting distracted her, and she was not fast enough. Liam let out a triumphant shout and held up a delicate calotte, a closefitting feathered skullcap as red as blood.

The merrow was enraged, and in her fury, her face twisted and changed and became as terrible as it had been lovely. "Give it to me!" she hissed, her long webbed fingers reaching for the calotte.

"If you want it, and with it your power to swim beneath the waves," Liam said, holding it just out of her grasp, "you must release the swans." I was amazed that he did not flinch before the merrow's wrath. I was frightened myself, for as she grew angrier, the lake began to take on a strange dark look and smell, like molten metal. When a stiff breeze stirred the water into whitecaps, I shivered in the sudden cold.

"Release them!" Liam shouted into the wind, which was blowing stronger now. "Release them, or I shall burn the cap!"

The merrow shrieked in anger and dread. "No!" she wailed. "Do not burn it! I release them—give me the calotte!" She stretched out her webbed hand again, and the swans, suddenly set free, were pushed back into the lake by the force of the springwater. Quickly they paddled into the reeds at the edge, taking shelter from the wild storm of wind and water.

"Give it to her!" Riona cried, her dark curls whipping across her face, and Liam held out the cap. His hand and the merrow's touched briefly, and I watched in horror as his skin blistered as if he had plunged it in fire.

The merrow placed the calotte on her head. As we stared, astonished, her feet beneath her silver gown seemed to fuse together, and in just an instant, from waist to toe she had become a scaled fishlike creature. She slipped from the mossy rocks into the water of the spring, gave a strong thrust with her fish tail, and disappeared into the mouth of the cave that led to Faerie.

The Escape:
And Where They Went

Neither Liam nor I was close enough to catch Riona as she collapsed, drained by the intensity of her struggle with the merrow. My breath seized in my throat as we ran to her and I saw how pale she was. But in a moment her eyes fluttered open, and she smiled weakly at us.

"Oh, Liam," she whispered, "however did you remember the calotte?"

We helped Riona to her feet, where she wobbled uncertainly.

"Don't you recall Mother's tales?" Liam asked, supporting her with an arm around her shoulder. He explained to me, "When we were small she told us about merrows—only her stories were always about the males, with their horrible green skin and red feather caps. Without their caps, she said, they are doomed to keep their human shapes and cannot return to Faerie. The tales gave me nightmares, so I never forgot them."

"I remember now," Riona murmured.

Let me see your hand, I said silently to Liam. He held it out. Red and blistered where he had touched the merrow, it looked even worse than my hands did. His fingers must have hurt terribly, but Liam did not flinch as I cradled them.

A paste of aloe and comfrey? I asked Riona.

"Exactly right," she replied, her voice stronger now, and I could not help feeling a touch of pride. "You have been learning as you spun and wove, Meriel!"

Dusk was coming on as we made our way as swiftly as we could back around the lake. I did not want to be anywhere near the Faerie spring when darkness fell. My brothers awaited us at the path. Thankful to see them safe, I ran ahead, and as they crowded around me, I tried to hug them all at once.

"You must stay away from the spring," Riona warned them. "The queen is not here, but her powers are working against us. Beware!"

The swans nodded and clapped their beaks to signal their understanding. Quickly I gathered up my bundle of cloth, but before I left, I went to Liam and touched his injured hand again gently. *You were very brave,* I told him, and he flushed with pleasure. Then I bade farewell to my brothers, calling silently as always, *Behave yourself when I am gone!* to Cullan though I knew he could not hear me.

I was dreadfully tired walking up the hill toward the castle. As I approached, I saw a flash of red—one of Lady Orianna's dreadful guards. I ducked behind a bush, my heart hammering, and watched him march about, too swollen with self-importance to notice me. As soon as he was out of sight, I ran to the vine and scrambled, exhausted, up and in through Cullan's window.

I dared not stop working. Mistress Tuileach brought broth and toast to my bedchamber, and as I told her of the merrow and her feather cap, she showed me how to cut and pin the cloth I had woven to make it into shirts.

"A merrow?" she marveled. "I have heard of such things, though I thought they were only sea creatures."

Obviously not, I said, silently but tartly, as I began my clumsy work as a seamstress.

"And a spring from Faerie, just as the stories say! I wonder . . ."

What?

She shook her head, but I knew what she wondered. What other menaces could Lady Orianna summon from the lands beneath the earth? I shivered, and my sudden movement caused me to jab my finger with the needle. The shirt I was sewing was quickly spotted with my blood. I kept trying to make my stitches as straight as I could, but the results were laughable, with uneven seams and zigzag hems. After the physical toil of reaping, spinning, and weaving, the drudgery of sewing together the pieces of fabric was a torment to me. My eyes soon grew weary and my back stiff from bending over my work. Oh, how I hated it!

When I could do no more, I slept for a few hours, but I woke, startled, to Mistress Tuileach shaking me.

"The king and queen are back!" she told me, her high brow creased with dismay.

Already? But why? I asked her, frightened.

"I do not know," Mistress Tuileach replied grimly. "But I believe that your resolve to stay silent may be sorely tested today."

In a panic I flew out of bed, scrabbling for my clothes.

But I cannot speak! I cried mutely. *My words will kill my brothers!*

"I know," Mistress Tuileach said. "I will help you in any way I can."

I ran to her then and threw my arms around her. Her embrace was warm and reassuring. *Thank you*, I told her. *I don't know what I would do without you.*

The day had dawned gray and threatening, and there was a chill in the air that clung to the stone walls of the castle despite the fires on every hearth. It was only late October, very early for weather this cold. Through the windows I could see a frost on the fields, the first hint of winter to come. I could not help thinking of Heart Lake, surely rimmed now with ice.

I was summoned soon after breakfast, and Mistress Tuileach came with me to the throne room, where the roaring fire did little to dispel the cold that rose through my thin shoes from the marble floor. Father and the queen sat in splendor, their courtiers ranged around them. We approached, then dipped in low curtsies.

"Well!" Father said, smiling at me. "You are up and about, daughter! Are you quite well at last?"

I nodded forcefully, smiling back at him. I wondered that he did not mark my red eyes, tired and swollen from a night of sewing. I could tell that the queen was staring at me, but I did my best to avoid meeting her gaze lest she read my thoughts.

"Your stepmother was not happy to be away from you when you were ill," Father continued, "so we concluded our business at once and hurried back. We are very relieved to see you recovered."

I curtsied in the queen's direction without meeting her eyes, and smiled again.

Mistress Tuileach hurried to fill my silence. "The princess is greatly improved, Your Majesty, though we are still trying not to strain her delicate throat." I tried to look as delicate as I could manage.

"Very wise," Father declared. "Now, Meriel, your stepmother the queen has had a marvelous idea, which she conveyed to me on the journey back." I exchanged a nervous look with Mistress Tuileach as he went on. "She feels that your education may have been somewhat . . . neglected. This is, of course, not a criticism of you, Mistress Tuileach, for there is only so much a governess can do."

"Yes, Your Majesty," Mistress Tuileach murmured.

"We believe that it would be best if Princess Meriel were to go away to school."

I looked at Father, horrified.

"Indeed," Lady Orianna inserted smoothly, "I myself was schooled at Madame Clodagh's School for Young Ladies of Nobility, and I know they would be honored to have you as a student. It is a beautiful place, on the coast in a very natural and isolated setting. Their instructors are of the highest quality. And there, my dear, you would learn all things necessary and appropriate to your rank."

No! No! I wanted to scream. I clapped a hand to my mouth to keep the words back, but Lady Orianna heard them as clearly as if I had shouted them aloud, and she smiled a terrible smile. She knew I could not protest, and that Father would take my silence for acceptance.

I tried to catch Father's eye. Surely he would not allow me to be sent away if he knew how I felt! But his expression was so complacent, his eyes so blank and dull. He could not see the distress written on my face at all. He was too deep in the queen's thrall. *It is not betrayal,* I told myself. *He cannot help it.*

I felt Mistress Tuileach's light touch on my shoulder, and I held myself very still.

"I shall get the princess's belongings ready for travel," Mistress Tuileach said. "When does she depart?"

"Tomorrow," Lady Orianna said lightly. "Parting will be difficult enough; it is best not to draw these things out. And your services, of course, will no longer be needed."

Mistress Tuileach bowed her head. She curtsied once more, her hand pushing me into a curtsy as well. And then we fled the throne room.

Back in my bedchamber, I paced back and forth like a caged beast. *What shall I do?* I implored Mistress

Tuileach. *I cannot abandon my brothers. There is no one else to help them!*

"You must leave this place," she answered as she pulled out two leather satchels from my closet.

Yes, I realized. *We will go to Riona and Liam. They will take us in.*

"The queen will search for you," Mistress Tuileach warned.

Their cottage is hidden, well off the main road, I told her. *You and I will be safe there—for a time.*

"No, Princess, I cannot go with you," Mistress Tuileach said gently. "I will go elsewhere, to throw her off the scent. She will expect us to be together, for I believe that she sees me truly now, and knows what I am."

Oh, Mistress Tuileach, I said mournfully. But I knew she was right. It was better for us both—and for my brothers, and Riona and Liam—if we were separated.

We packed a satchel for each of us and hid them away, and then I spent the day sewing and sewing as Mistress Tuileach folded my clothes and placed them in great traveling trunks to be sent to the school where I would not follow. I thought regretfully of my brothers, waiting for me all day at the lake, and of Riona and Liam. They would wonder where I was, but I knew they would be wise enough to stay away from the castle.

Do you think, I asked Mistress Tuileach as I stitched,

that Lady Orianna really plans to send me to school, or does she intend to turn me into a bird as she did my brothers? Or something worse, perhaps—an eel? Or a horrid sightless mole?

"I don't know, Princess," Mistress Tuileach admitted. "But I think it would not be a good idea to wait and find out."

When evening fell, we ate together in my bedchamber. Then I rolled up the shirts and pushed them and my pincushion and thimble into my satchel, and we crept out of the room and down the hall to Cullan's bedchamber. I opened the window and pointed out the thick vine to Mistress Tuileach. She whispered, "Take care, child!" before I lowered myself, hand over hand, to the ground. Mistress Tuileach tossed the satchels to me; mine was light and I caught it handily, but hers knocked me right over.

What do you have in there? I asked her, irritated, as I picked myself up.

She gripped the vine and whispered back, "One cannot leave one's favorite books, Princess!" The ivy swayed and she gasped as she climbed down the vine, inch by painful inch. At last she reached the bottom, where she stood motionless for a moment to regain her composure.

"I am far too old for such goings-on," she muttered, picking up her bag.

You are not old in the least, I assured her. Indeed, in the cold moonlight—for the clouds had blown away—with her face flushed from exertion, she looked almost young and very nearly pretty.

As we headed toward the lane, a figure stepped out of the shadows, and I stopped, my heart beating wildly. The moonlight shone on the red jacket and gold epaulets of a guard, and for a moment I thought all was lost. Then I realized it was Ogan, and I breathed again.

"Princess!" he said, very low. "I must tell you that you are in great danger."

Mistress Tuileach looked at me, and I said to her, *We can trust him. He is one of ours.*

Mistress Tuileach spoke for me. "We know the queen's intentions, young sir," she said. "We are fleeing for our very lives."

"You do not know it all," Ogan said softly. "I have overheard something."

"What is it?" Mistress Tuileach asked.

He looked around nervously, then said, "The queen was speaking to one of her own men. I walked past with a company of guards, and she did not realize I wasn't one of hers. I heard her say . . ." His voice, dismayed, trailed off.

"Speak, boy!" Mistress Tuileach demanded in a low tone.

"She described a pact she has made with the creatures of Faerie. She intends to have a son and put him on the throne. She did not say what would happen to the king, but I imagine . . ." Again he stopped speaking, and I began to tremble.

"Go on," Mistress Tuileach insisted.

"Under her son's reign, the doors between the lands below and our lands will be opened. All of Faerie will come aboveground, and they will rule us."

My eyes widened in alarm, and Mistress Tuileach gasped with shock.

"Her guards know her wicked intention and will help her," Ogan continued. "I think some of them are not even human. Princess, I fear she has killed your brothers, and will kill you as well if she can."

"Guard," Mistress Tuileach told him, "the princes are not dead, and Princess Meriel is working to save them."

Ogan looked astonished, and Mistress Tuileach said, "I will not tell you more, for it is dangerous for you to have that knowledge. But your words help us, for now we know all. Before, we were not clear about her intention, and so we did not know the full danger. We are grateful to you." Ogan bowed, and she went on, "If you dare to stay here, you must guard your thoughts around the queen, for she can hear them as clearly as if you speak them. Do not let her know what you know, if you value your life."

"If the princess needs me, I will be here," he vowed. "If I can, I will be her ears inside the castle, and for her sake, I will take care." I curtsied low to him, and he bowed again before turning back to the castle.

At the first branch in the lane Mistress Tuileach and I parted. She hugged me hard and I wept a little, clutching her. "Do not despair, Princess," she said tenderly. "I have the utmost confidence in you. And do not forget this: your love for your brothers is your greatest power."

I shall not forget, I promised her.

"Until we meet again, then," she said, and pressed a kiss on my brow. I watched her walk away until the night swallowed her up. Then I continued on my way.

I was ever ready to leap off the lane into a ditch should anyone appear, but even with the moonlight it was dark and very cold, and all wise travelers were indoors by their fires. No one passed me as I walked, and I quickly reached Riona and Liam's cottage. Liam opened the door to my soft knock, his expression greatly surprised. His hand was wrapped in a bandage.

"Meriel!" he exclaimed, stepping aside to let me in. "Why are you out at this hour? And why did you not come to the lake today? We were worried—what's happened?"

I warmed my hands by the fire as Riona brought me hot tea and bade me sit and be welcome. The rabbit hopped from his favorite nook and sat beside me. Numbly, I told of the queen's plan to send me off to school, and then related what Ogan had overheard.

"It all makes sense," Riona murmured. "Even now, the doors between Faerie and our lands are opening. In town, the blacksmith said he'd seen a púca—do you know what that is?"

It is a kind of ghost, isn't it? I asked.

"Yes, ghostlike and shape-shifting both. He saw it as a black horse with golden eyes. It frightened him terribly."

Liam added, "He said the púca tried to get him to ride it. If he had . . . well, we would not have seen him again."

And this is the queen's doing?

"I do not know," Riona admitted. "But it seems that the world below is coming closer to us, and if she has sworn to open those doors . . ." She shuddered, and I did too.

I cannot go back to the castle. I have nowhere else to go, I admitted. *May I stay with you?*

"Of course you must stay here!" Riona assured me.

"We can keep you hidden, for a time at least. But you cannot go out."

No, I said to her regretfully. *I cannot see my brothers, and you should not either, for the queen knows you.*

"I can visit them," Liam pointed out. "She doesn't know me. I'll go to the lake each day and tell them how you fare, and I can report on them to you." I turned grateful eyes to him, and he gave me his quick sweet grin. I was growing very fond of that grin.

"Let me bring your bag upstairs," he said. "Riona can show you where you'll stay."

I rose, and we climbed the narrow staircase to the floor above, low ceilinged under the slanted roof. There were three closed doors at the top of the stair, two that I guessed opened to Liam's and their mother's rooms and one that Riona opened to reveal her bedchamber.

"We will have to share," Riona said apologetically. I gazed around at the tiny space. A white-painted iron bedstead stood before the window, and there was room only for a simple oak chest and a little table besides. I thought of my own bedchamber, enormous compared to this. For a moment I wondered why they did not put me in their mother's room, giving me some privacy. Then I realized that sharing the little room with Riona would be a hundred times nicer than being alone in the other room, and a thousand times nicer than being in my own lonely bedchamber, with the queen lurking downstairs and only Mistress Tuileach for company.

This will be very cozy, I said with approval. Liam grinned again, setting my satchel atop the wooden chest.

"We'll leave you to get settled," Riona said. "Come down when you are ready; I've made some soup."

They clattered down the stairs, and I unpacked my few belongings, glad that I had brought so little. Even so, my silver comb and mirror looked gaudy atop the little table, and I pushed them into the chest with my extra overdress. As I laid my nightdress on the bed, I heard the sound of footsteps outside, and my heart leaped. The bedchamber was under the eaves in the front of the cottage, so its window looked out on the path that led to the front door. I squeezed by the bed, and standing to the side so I could not be seen from without, I peered through the window.

A woman was coming up the path. In the moonlight I could see that she was cloaked, but her hood was pulled up against the cold, so I could not make out her face. I sagged against the wall in terror. Had Lady Orianna learned of my disappearance already? How could she have found me so quickly?

There was a pounding at the front door, and I bit down on my knuckle to keep from crying out. Liam's boots were loud as he walked across the front room, and quick as a flash I dove beneath the iron bedstand. Then I remembered my satchel holding the nettle shirts, open on top of the chest, and I scrambled back out to grab it. I pushed my nightdress inside as well. Clutching the satchel to me, I scurried back under the bed. A sudden movement at my feet made me gasp, and the stoat slithered up to settle itself beside me, its black eyes gazing into mine. There we waited, the stoat and I, my heart hammering in my ears, as I heard Liam open the door.

The Fire:
And What Was Destroyed

Mother!" Liam cried from downstairs, his voice joyful, and I heard Riona echo him: "Mother! You've returned!"

I lay limp with relief on the dusty floor beneath the bed. I could not move. The rush of fear and then its disappearance had left me utterly weakened. Even when I heard Liam dash up the staircase and open the door to the bedchamber, I could not stir.

"Meriel?" he said, confused when he did not see me. Then he bent down, and his face came into view.

"What on earth are you doing?" he asked, his blue eyes amused. "Is this a time for hide-and-seek?"

I scowled at him, willing my trembling limbs to push me out. Then I saw understanding in his face.

"Ah," he said in sympathy. "You thought it was the queen. No wonder you were frightened! But it is just our mother, home at last, kicking at the door because she had no hand free to open it."

I was not frightened in the least, I retorted crossly, my pride giving me the strength to crawl from my hiding place. I stirred up dust as I moved, and it made me sneeze violently. The stoat sneezed as well, and Liam started to laugh as I struggled to stand. "We are not the best housekeepers," he admitted. "Especially when Mother is away."

I ignored him as I brushed the dust from my skirt, trying to preserve what remained of my dignity. When the stoat and I both sneezed again, though, I started to laugh with Liam, keeping my giggles silent as my shoulders heaved. It felt so good to be merry, after all the days of work and worry!

Finally Liam wiped his eyes and bent to pick up the stoat, which was grooming the dust off its shiny fur. "Come down and meet Mother," he said, placing the stoat on his shoulder. "She knows all about you and is very eager to make your acquaintance."

Knows all about me? How? I asked him, following him down the narrow stair.

"Well, she's a *witch*, Meriel," he pointed out, and I had to suppress another laugh.

In the main room, Liam and Riona's mother was bustling about, plumping up a cushion here, straightening a curtain there. She stopped when she saw me and came forward to take my hands in hers. She was a short, round woman with the same dark curls and azure eyes as her children. Her dress, like her daughter's, was undyed linen, and she wore a string of aromatic herbs around her neck. The pockets of her apron were stuffed with dried plants, and a lovely scent of sage and lavender rose from her. Her cheeks were red from the cold, but her hands were warm, and her greeting was warmer still.

"Princess Meriel, welcome to our home!" she exclaimed. "I am Brigh, the mother of these two wild things." She motioned to Riona and Liam, who made faces of embarrassment. "Your Highness, I met your governess on the road to Corbrack. We had a quick cup of tea at an inn there, and spoke of your troubles." She turned my palms upward and looked at their ruddy roughness. I saw great sympathy in her expression. "How you have struggled, poor dear!"

Is Mistress Tuileach well? I asked her silently, and she heard me clearly.

"Yes, child, she is well enough, but worried for you. I had not known her before, but—well, like recognizes like, you know!" She beamed at me and went on, "When she learned who I was, she told me all. Oh, your task is formidable, my dear! And you keep at it, though I can see it has caused you much suffering."

I pulled back my hands and shrugged. *It has not been so bad,* I said.

"Ah, your governess said you were brave! She told me of the queen and her enchantment, and her fearsome plan. I had already heard of the lady Orianna. Your stepmother is legendary in our circles—this is not her first wicked act!"

No? I said with great interest. *What else has she done?*

Brigh pulled me to the chairs by the crackling fire, and we sat. Liam brought me my sewing, and I began stitching. Liam and Riona sprawled on the rug beside us, and the rabbit hopped around them.

"Well," Brigh said, "she was thwarted in love, they say. This was very long ago, for she is far older than she looks! So are we all, we witches." Her eyes twinkled. "The unlucky prince who did not choose her for a wife—no one knows just what became of him. The stories say that she placed him on an enchanted isle, where he wanders to this day weeping for her and calling out her name. It is clear she is a woman who is dangerous to cross!"

I shuddered to imagine the poor prince, pacing his lonely island and calling hopelessly for Lady Orianna. *Will she find me here?* I asked nervously, stitching away.

"I can help protect you, I think," said Brigh. "You are safer here than most other places, at any rate."

That was not especially comforting to hear, but I was distracted from my worries by the sight of the rabbit nose to nose with a small cat face that peeked out from beneath Brigh's skirts.

Is that one of yours? I asked Liam. He shook his head.

"I help the wild animals," he said. "A cat is a pet—or a familiar. And a terrible cliché in this household. Really, Mother!"

Brigh smiled, reaching down to lift the cat—no more than a kitten, really—into her lap. "Ah, but this one was wounded. A thorn in its paw, like the lion that Androcles found. I couldn't leave it to suffer, could I?" She leaned toward me and said in a confidential tone, "My son will not name any of his animals, for he says they all have their own forest or meadow names, and it is not our place to give them new ones. But I have named them all." She pointed to each in turn. "The rabbit is Coinin, the stoat I call Easog, the thrush is Molach, and Madame Crow is Macha. But my cat, dear tabby, is just called Catkin."

The kitten meowed as if replying, and I wondered if it actually was a familiar, a witch's helper, rather than just an ordinary cat.

We talked, and I sewed until I was too tired to see my stitches. I had now finished two of the five shirts, and I held them up to admire my work. Liam snorted at the first. It had one sleeve considerably longer than the other and barely looked like clothing at all, but the second was better—quite recognizably a shirt.

That night I slept restlessly beside Riona, unused to sharing a bed. I rose at the song of Molach the thrush and sewed on, pricking my fingers just a little. The day passed quietly; toward evening, Liam came back from Tiramore, where he had been doctoring a mare in labor. His face was somber as he hung his cloak, and he sat beside me and said, "Meriel, they are looking for you in town. The queen's guards have marched up and down every street and knocked at every door."

I raised troubled eyes to his. *What did the townspeople do?* I asked.

"They are your people, Meriel. They do not like the queen and seem to know she is not to be trusted. Some ordered the guards from their shops and homes, and none would speak of you. Nowhere were they given any aid at all."

Oh, I said in wonder. I had not spent very much time

in Tiramore, and I did not know the people. I did not think they knew me. It was gratifying to hear that they esteemed me enough to protect me as they had.

As the hour grew late, Brigh said, "Children, get your cloaks. I wish to show you something."

I looked inquiringly at Liam, but he shrugged. I laid aside my sewing, took my cloak from a peg beside the door, and followed the others out into the darkness. Our breath plumed in the cold air, and the full moon hung low, enormous and orange in the night sky.

In silence we walked, and I realized before long that we were heading to Heart Lake. I hurried ahead and put my hand on Brigh's arm to stop her.

It is not safe, I warned her. *The lake is fed with a spring from Faerie, and my stepmother has already summoned a merrow from its depths. She may have placed guards there as well.*

"I know, my dear," she replied. "Riona told me of the merrow. But we will only be there for a short time and will stay far from the spring. It sounds for now as if the guards are busy in town. If we see them, we will turn back. I think you will be glad at what I have to show you." She would not say more.

We approached the lake as the moon rose higher, casting a silver trail across the water. Close to shore I could see the swans, grouped together. They swam toward the moon trail, and when the first swan was touched by moonlight, its feathers dropped away and the bird's form lengthened and changed. As I watched in astonishment, I saw my brother Darrock standing before me, up to his booted ankles in lake water. Then Cullan changed from bird to man, then Aidan, Baird, and Druce. In an instant they were all there: my five brothers in human form, like phantoms in the mist. Could they be real?

Riona cried out as I could not, and we both ran forward to the lake's edge. I threw my arms around Darrock and felt his warm embrace. "Your courage astounds me, sister!" he whispered before handing me to Aidan, who squeezed the breath out of me. I hugged Druce and Baird, and they murmured praise, and next I turned to Cullan, whose arms were tight around Riona. I glanced at Brigh and saw surprise on her face. Then Cullan released Riona and grabbed me and twirled me about, the icy water splashing about our legs.

"Well done thus far, little one!" he said, and my joy nearly overwhelmed me. But at that moment a cloud crossed the moon, and its silver trail disappeared. Without warning Cullan dropped me into the water. My brothers shrank and altered and were befeathered. All at once there were five swans swimming where just an instant before there had been five young men standing.

Riona's eyes filled with tears. "What has happened?"

"It was the full moon, my love," her mother explained. "At midnight on the night of the full moon, when the orb's light falls on the enchanted one, the spell is lifted—but only for a moment."

"It is almost worse to see him again," Riona mourned.

"Oh, child," Brigh said gently, "I did not know you loved him. He is a prince, and you are the daughter of a witch and a sailor. Is this wise?"

Riona wiped her eyes and stood very straight. "The heart has its own wisdom, Mother," she replied.

Then suddenly a silken voice that nearly made my heart stop came from up the path. "And what better husband for a sailor's child than a waterbird?" The clouds parted enough for the moon to show us the form of Lady Orianna, standing before us in a fur-trimmed green cloak. Behind her were two of her guards, their hands on their swords.

I shrank back and Liam stepped bravely in front of me, but Brigh said calmly, "Welcome, Your Majesty. Have you come to see your handiwork?"

The queen's face was hidden beneath her hood. I imagined her scowl, though, and her annoyance was clear in her voice when she answered, "I do not know you, woman, but I see my stepdaughter by your side. We have been much concerned over her absence. Come,

Meriel." She beckoned to me, and the moonlight glinted off the ruby ring that my father had given her.

I will not! I told her, silent but defiant.

"I say you will." Lady Orianna stepped forward, seeming to grow taller and more menacing as she approached. I felt rooted to the ground; my legs would not move. On the water my brothers began to flap their wings wildly, and the queen was momentarily distracted by the commotion. When her attention wavered, I was free to turn, and I sprinted away, back down the path. I could hear footsteps following me and hoped desperately that Liam and Riona were following me, not the guards. Then I heard two voices, Brigh's and the queen's, raised in anger, speaking strange rhyming words that I knew were spells.

As the path curved away, I glanced over my shoulder. Liam and Riona were just behind me, and above the spot where the two witches stood hurling incantations, an unearthly greenish light glimmered in the sky and was reflected in the water. Sparks flew from it and landed, hissing, on the surface of the lake.

My shoe caught on a root and I pitched forward. Liam caught me just before I went down, and he kept a firm grip on my arm as we dashed down the dark lane and turned off onto the path to the cottage. But another light glowed there, and it was not the cheery radiance of candles in the window. It was the crackling glare of fire.

"Our cottage!" Riona cried out in despair. Liam let go of me and raced ahead, throwing open the front door and disappearing inside. "Liam!" his sister screamed. "Come back! Save yourself!"

I sank to the cold ground, shaking, my hands over my mouth. Riona ran up to the door, but the blaze pushed her back. She darted from window to window, trying to see inside, but there were only smoke and flame.

I have brought this on you, I thought, weeping. *I have killed Liam! Oh, forgive me!* But Riona did not hear me or chose not to answer. She ran around to the back of the cottage, and I scrambled up and followed her.

As we reached the garden, a beam in the cottage gave way, and with a groan and a crash the roof fell in. Sparks soared upward like a thousand fireflies, as they had flown above the two witches at the lake. Again Riona screamed in horror. I thought she would collapse and reached out to hold her up.

And then we saw him amidst the brown and wilted garden plants—Liam, alive and unburned. His face was streaked with ash, and his hair was singed, but in his arms was Catkin and on each shoulder a trembling bird. The stunned faces of Coinin and Easog, the rabbit and stoat, peeped from a sack he carried. All living, all unharmed. We stared, unbelieving, and then Riona did faint, falling in a heap before I could grab her.

I crouched beside her and patted her cheeks gently to rouse her, and Liam knelt too, the birds clinging to him fearfully with their claws.

"Sister!" Liam said, his voice hoarse from smoke. Riona's eyes fluttered open, and reassured, he joked, "You have become quite the lady, fainting at every little thing!"

She stared blankly at him, as if she could not believe he was truly there. Then she smiled with relief. "Yes, Brother," she replied, her trembling voice belying her calm words, "you are right. A battle with a merrow, and my childhood home burned to the ground—mere inconveniences. I shall have to toughen up!" She struggled to her feet and then bent to pet Catkin as we gazed at the remains of the cottage, utterly engulfed now in flames. The heat was intense enough to force us backward into the garden.

Forgive me, I said again numbly.

Riona turned to me. There was no anger or blame in her expression. "Oh, Meriel," she said sadly, "this is not your fault. It was the queen's doing, I am sure of it. And everything of real value was saved, thanks to my brother's recklessness."

"Recklessness?" Liam repeated, offended. "I showed

the courage of a hero of old! You should bow before me!"

But I did not smile, for Riona's words echoed inside me. *Everything of real value was saved.* The animals, yes, and Liam, thank goodness. But the shirts that I had struggled so to make were still inside, and they were now nothing more than ash. The thrush and crow, the rabbit, stoat, cat, and Liam were alive, but the shirts were burned, and so my brothers all were doomed.

10

The Apothecary:
And How He Helped

A s I stood in utter despair, I did not hear Liam at first over the roar of the fire. "Look, Meriel!" he shouted, and then even louder, "Meriel, look!" He scooped the rabbit and stoat from his sack and pulled out a length of cloth, then another and another, and at last my two finished shirts. "I have them!" he crowed, his triumphant face lit fantastically by the dancing flames.

I could not speak, even silently. I reached out and touched the rough fabric, and then I reached farther and clutched Liam to me. The birds fluttered from his shoulders to the ground, squawking with dismay as I burst into tears again.

I do bow before you! I said, sobbing, and started to release him to do just that. But he held me tighter.

"No, this will do very well," he told me. My thoughts raced wildly in my head. *His arms are very strong,* I thought, and *How can he joke when his home is destroyed?* And absurdly, *I must look a terrible mess!* When at last his grip loosened, he gazed down at me and smiled.

"You look fine for a girl who has been chased by a witch," he said. I hiccupped and wiped my face with my sleeve.

You, on the other hand, do not appear entirely fresh, I pointed out. The bandage on his hand was dark with soot, and his shirt had half a dozen holes where embers must have landed. But he was every inch the hero to me.

"Children, children, where are you?" came a frantic call from the darkness, and Brigh emerged into the firelight. Her face was drawn and anguished. When she saw us, though, she cried out with joy and ran to pull all three of us into her warm embrace.

"My darlings, when I saw the flames . . . ," she began, but she could not go on.

"We are all right, Mother," Riona assured her. "Liam has rescued Meriel's shirts—and all the animals as well."

"Oh, bravely done, Son!" Brigh exclaimed, planting a kiss on Liam's filthy cheek. Even in the dimness I could see his face flush.

"But the queen, Mother—what has become of her?" Riona pressed.

"I did my best," Brigh told us. "I held her off and wore her out, but she will come back as strong, or stronger. And she had the power to do this while we battled." She indicated the wreck of the cottage. "We must go away from here. She must not find us."

"Where will we go?" Liam asked, pushing my shirts back into the sack and looking around for the animals.

"To town," Brigh replied, "and quickly. We have friends there—they will take us in and hide us."

We were nearly too exhausted to stand, but Brigh herded us through the meadows to Tiramore. We did not dare take the road. We climbed wearily over stiles and fences and crossed fields crusted with frost. The horizon began to lighten as we approached town, but the inhabitants still slept.

Tiramore was encircled with a high stone wall, built in the days when Castle Rua was a stronghold against invaders. Its front gate, once made of thick timbers and watched by two soldiers, was unguarded now. The lane from the castle ran into town through the gate and became the high street, leading to the market square in the town's center. From there other smaller streets radiated outward in all directions, so that the market square was like the center of a wheel and the streets like its spokes. After checking to be sure no one was about, Brigh urged us through the gate and along the high street, and we stopped before a small apothecary shop near the square. A brightly painted sign showing a mortar and pestle hung above it, and in the many-paned front window there were glass balls filled with red and blue fluids.

Brigh knocked lightly on the door, two quick raps and then three more. In a minute we saw a light in an upstairs window, then heard steps on the stair. The door opened to reveal a red-faced, jowly man wearing a nightcap and carrying a candle.

"Madame Brigh?" he said, his voice sleep fuzzed. "It is very early for a consultation, you know!" Then he took in the sight of us and stepped back quickly. "Come in," he urged. "Goodness gracious, whatever has happened? You look as though you'd been to war!"

"We very nearly have been, Master Declan," Brigh said wearily as we passed into the shop. The candle's light revealed a long wooden counter that ran from one end of the shop to the other. There were scales and weights of brass and silver on it, and behind the counter were shelves that rose to the ceiling. I gazed around in wonder. The lower shelves held beautiful blue and white porcelain jars, each with a label. Bottles and flasks filled with liquids in every color lined the next shelves. And still higher up were large glass vessels with strange, terrible objects suspended in cloudy substances—objects that I could not identify and did not dare to guess at. The smell of spices sweet and hot, fresh and musty quite overwhelmed the senses.

"You've never been in here before?" Liam asked, joining me as I walked about, peering at labels and jars of liniment.

I have never gone to any shop, I told him. *Princesses don't. Dressmakers and cobblers come to me, and other items just . . . appear. And we have our own doctor, though he is quite useless.*

"Useless?" Liam asked.

He can only bleed and cup his patients, which never seems to do any good. He would no more know that buckthorn bark cures gout than that—well, that nettles can be spun into thread.

Liam grinned, his teeth white against his sooty skin. "In future, then, you should have Mother and Riona tend to sickness at the castle."

In future . . . I did not dare imagine the future.

The apothecary led us upstairs to his family's living quarters, where we met his stout, cheery wife Eveleen, and their children, Davina and Ennis, both light haired and blue eyed like their mother. Davina was a tiny thing, around six years old. When she saw Liam's menagerie she was enthralled, and immediately she and Coinin the rabbit became fast friends. Ennis was nearly grown and very handsome, with blond hair that fell over one eye. It was clear that he was already well acquainted with Riona. More than once I caught him gazing at her with an expression that seemed far beyond friendship, and I wondered if he knew of her feelings for Cullan.

Brigh described our plight to Master Declan and his family, with frequent interruptions of "Goodness gracious!" from the apothecary.

"You and your children can stay in our examination room downstairs tonight, Madame Brigh," the apothecary's wife said. "The princess can have our chamber, though I fear it will not be very comfortable."

I shook my head insistently. *Tell them no!* I thought at Brigh. *I shall stay below with you.*

Brigh relayed my wishes, and little Davina turned to me, her eyes bright with curiosity.

"Why don't you speak, Your Highness? Can't you speak? Why not? I would like to know what it is like to be a princess. Will you tell me? Please?"

Madame Eveleen flushed with embarrassment and tried to silence her daughter, but Brigh and Liam and Riona laughed, and I smiled too.

"The princess cannot speak," Brigh told Davina. "But you may sit with her as she sews, if your mother will allow."

"Oh, Mama, may I? Please? Do say that I may!" The child danced back and forth with excitement.

Her mother granted permission, as long as Davina was quiet, adding, "But you must not tell anyone that you have met the princess, or that she is staying with us."

"No, I promise, I will not stay a word!" Davina pledged, overjoyed.

We washed off the soot from the fire and then slept for a bit in the family's beds upstairs, while they opened the shop for the day and treated customers. When I woke, I began my sewing again, sitting with Brigh, Riona, and Liam in the comfortable main room beside the fire. I listened to the commerce below as I stitched. A bell attached to the door rang each time a customer entered, and patients described their ailments to the apothecary, from a sore toe to a rash, a dry cough to a toothache. For each Master Declan mixed a potion or created a tincture from the herbs and liquids on his shelves. From time to time he took a patient into the back room to examine. All received a treatment, and all left the shop pleased.

His work is very like yours, then, I said to Brigh.

"Yes," she said softly, so we could not be heard below. "We often work together. Many of his herbs come from my garden. But I go to the places where there is no apothecary, or where the patient is too ill or too badly hurt to come here."

Davina ran up and down the stairs all day, whispering loudly to us of her doings. Ennis, who helped his father with the more practical business of the shop, came up at every opportunity to sit beside Riona and talk quietly. Sewing in the corner, I saw how his eyes never strayed from her face as they spoke. They'd forgotten that I was there when I heard Riona say, "But I did not make a promise to you, Ennis."

I almost forgot to breathe as I waited for his answer. It was long in coming and low. "It was understood. I thought it was understood."

Riona's voice trembled. "We have always been friends. You never said—I—" She stopped herself and reached for his hand. "Ennis, I have grown to love another. I love you as a brother, but this man . . . it is different."

Ennis snorted and pulled his hand away. "A brother! That is what every suitor longs to hear, to be sure. And do you think I don't know the name of your beloved? The whole town knows, and they laugh at you for it. A penniless half-witch, and a prince of the realm—it is absurd!"

"That is beneath you, Ennis," Riona said coolly, and she turned away from him. Her eyes met mine, and I lowered my gaze to the shirt under my needle as Ennis stormed down the stairs and out of the shop.

As evening fell I stopped my sewing briefly to rest my stiff hands, and Master Declan closed the shop. His long white apron, spotless when he descended the stairs in the morning, was streaked with vivid colors and odd substances by the time he came back up, grunting with the effort, at suppertime. He brought me a tincture of sage for my strained eyes, and it soothed the ache. Then I went to the window and looked out at the life of the town below, which I had never had the chance to observe before. People passed to and fro, from butcher shop to cooper's, from blacksmith's to chandler's, finishing their day's errands. They met in the street with cries of pleasure, exchanged handshakes and kisses, stopped to chat and were on their way again. It was like watching a mummers' play, endlessly entertaining.

Liam joined me, and we gazed down at a young couple whose hands brushed as they walked up the street. I thought of how Ennis had brushed Riona's hand in just that way as they sat together, before they argued.

Do you know that the apothecary's son loves Riona? I asked him bluntly.

He nodded, still looking out the window. "Until last summer, we assumed they would marry," he said. "But then . . ."

Oh dear, I said, thinking of Cullan and his long, unfortunate history with girls.

"I probably should not ask you this, but . . . do you know your brother's intentions?" Liam's expression was intense.

I do not, I said regretfully. *But even before the enchantment, he seemed far more devoted to Riona than he had been to any other.*

Liam looked thoughtful. I gazed out the window for one more moment before resuming my work and noticed Davina below on the street. She was approaching a dog that wagged its dark tail as she came closer. The dog's ears were back against its skull, which I had never before seen in a tail-wagging dog. Usually our hunting dogs drew their ears back only when they were at the chase, or when they growled in anger. I looked closer as the animal turned its head and saw the glint of gold. Its eyes were gold.

Liam! I cried silently. *Look at that dog!*

Liam stared down at the street for an instant and then turned and ran. I hammered on the window as loudly as I could, hoping to catch Davina's attention, as Liam clattered down the stairs and out the shop door.

Just as Davina's hand reached out to pet the dog's silky fur, Liam grabbed her and spun her around. I could only see, not hear, what happened. Davina's mouth fell open in protest, and as she and Liam argued the dog— or whatever it was—slunk quietly down the high street and disappeared. It did not turn into an alleyway or doorway. It simply was and then was not.

Davina was still complaining as Liam hurried her back into the shop and up the stairs. "It was lost!" she insisted. "It was a lost dog and it wanted to come home with me, and how can you say you help animals? You let it stay lost! I was going to help it! Now it will starve to death!"

Liam took Davina's hands in his and said, very calmly, "It was not a dog."

Davina was silent with surprise, but only for a moment. "But it looked like a dog," she pointed out.

"Yes," Liam acknowledged, "but it was not. It was a púca."

Madame Eveleen came out from the kitchen when she heard that. "A púca!" she exclaimed. "Are they real, then?"

"Well—as real as any ghost is," Liam said. "I am sure that's what it was. It had golden eyes."

"And Davina—," Madame Eveleen began, a belated

look of alarm crossing her face.

"She did not touch it," Liam assured her. "It's gone now." He turned back to Davina. "You must stay away from animals you don't know," he instructed her. "Horses, goats, dogs, even rabbits. Do not touch them unless I say it's all right."

"Why?" Davina asked, ever curious. "What will happen if I do touch them?"

"I'm not sure," Liam admitted. "But I think it is best you don't find out. It . . . it might hurt."

Davina thought about this for a moment and then nodded. "I will ask you next time," she said to Liam, and he smiled at her. But the look he exchanged with me was anxious. The door to Faerie was opening wider.

That night, as we slept uncomfortably on pallets in the apothecary's examination room, flakes began to fall from the sky. By the time I awoke, the snow was ankle deep on the street outside the shop, and the air was frigid.

My brothers! I thought in a panic, leaping up. *The lake will be frozen!* I was still dressed in my clothes from the day before, so I pulled on my shoes and was halfway through the shop to the front door when Liam caught up with me.

"Where are you going, Meriel?" he demanded, trying to slow me with a hand on my arm.

To the lake! I cried mutely. *My brothers will freeze or fly away to save themselves. I must help them!*

"Let me go," Liam suggested swiftly. "You have to stay here and sew—and there may be guards. I will do what I can."

But I was frantic. I had to see for myself that they were still there. *Come with me, then,* I said, and we ran out of the shop.

The snow was a curtain of white, and we slipped and slid through it toward Heart Lake. There was no sign of the queen's soldiers, but when we came close, my spirits sank. The wide part of the lake that formed the two rounds of the heart was covered by a glaze of new ice. There was a slender corridor of open water leading to the tapered end, where the spring from Faerie fed the lake. My brothers paddled on that narrow path. It was clear that as the lake continued to freeze, they would be pushed closer and closer to the spring and whatever evils lurked below it.

We must break through the ice, I commanded Liam. *It can't be very thick yet. If we open up the water at this end, they won't be forced to swim toward the spring.*

I picked up a stone and stepped out onto the ice.

Liam gave me a doubtful look, but he found a heavy rock and moved gingerly after me. We pounded on the ice with our rocks, but it would not crack.

Carefully we made our way farther out onto the frozen lake, testing the weight of the ice with each footstep. The swans watched us intently.

Liam gave a great shout, raised his rock, and slammed it to the ice with a crash. For a moment nothing happened. Then the ice cracked, and he scuttled backward. Quickly cracks radiated outward from the place where the rock had landed, overtaking him as he tried to escape.

I leaped desperately toward the shore, and with one great jump landed on firm ground. But Liam had been out beyond me. As he scrabbled back, the ice disintegrated beneath him, and with a wild cry and a splash, he plunged into the water and disappeared below the surface.

Searching frantically, I grabbed a stick and tried to walk back out on the ice, but it shattered and I splashed ankle-deep into the lake. Instantly my toes went numb. I could see no sign of Liam in the open water, so I tried to get to the spot where he had fallen through the ice. From there to the place where I stood, the ice still remained, riddled with cracks but whole.

I threw myself full-length on it, hoping it would hold me, and, lying on my stomach, tried to inch out to the hole where Liam had disappeared. Then I looked down.

And to my utter horror, I saw just below me—beneath the ice I lay upon—Liam's upturned face.

11

The Chase:
And How They Fled

Liam's desperate eyes looked up into mine, with just a knuckle's thickness of ice between us. Frantically I hammered on the ice with my fists and my stick, and he hammered from below, but we could not break through.

All at once, I felt the brush of feathers on my neck. Three of my brothers were there beside me, their webbed feet slipping and sliding. They pushed me away and pounded on the ice with their hard beaks. The other two worked in the open water at the edge of the ice, shattering it with their strong wings. The three swans beside me quickly pecked a large enough hole that one of them—Aidan?—could reach down and grasp Liam's hair in his beak, pulling him upward.

As soon as Liam took a breath of air, he gave a wrenching gasp and began to cough and retch. It took only a few moments for the other swans to beat away enough of the ice to free him completely. With the aid of my stick—and my brothers pushing from behind—I pulled Liam to shore, and he sprawled nearly insensible on the ground, his matted curls freezing. He coughed and shivered so hard that I feared he would fly to pieces.

He had just begun to regain his breath when I heard a shout and looked up to see a contingent of the queen's guards in their red uniforms marching toward us. I pulled Liam to his feet, and we staggered back toward town, the guards gaining on us with every step. I supported his weight as well as I could. The second time we fell in the slippery snow, I wasn't sure I could get him up, but he struggled to his feet and stumbled onward.

As we neared Tiramore, I noticed a group of townspeople at the gate in the stone wall, watching us and pointing at the soldiers behind us.

Run! I cried silently to Liam. *The guards are almost upon us!*

I do not know how he did it, but Liam broke into a run, and I had to sprint to keep up with him. We dashed through the gate, and just inside the towns-people circled around, hiding us from view. They led us down the high street. I heard the sound of boots on cobblestones and did not dare glance at the shop windows as we sped toward the square.

It was market day, and despite the cold and snow, the marketplace was filled to overflowing. Buyers and sellers, dogs barking and snatching up dropped morsels of food, children playing hoops, mummers hoping for tossed coins from onlookers in payment for their performances—all turned to stare as we rushed by. Still surrounded, Liam and I wove through the makeshift wooden tables displaying the goods of late fall: honey, cabbages and potatoes and apples, braided breads and sweet cakes. It seemed to me—or was I imagining it?—that everyone we passed looked me straight in the eyes and smiled. Many mouthed the word "Courage!" But then I heard a voice shout, "Halt!" and I knew that the guards were fast upon us.

In my fear I stumbled and went down, dragging Liam with me, and as our protectors surged around us, we crawled beneath one of the tables ringing the square. We crouched there in terror. I breathed in the scent of cloves and cinnamon for sale above, trying to calm myself as the polished boots of the guards marched by. Then I heard one of them cry out, "There! Down that street!" I knew that voice. It was Ogan, and he was sending the men away from us.

When they were gone, we struggled out from beneath the table. Hands lifted us up and set us back on our feet. Then the townspeople led Liam and me down a cobbled street, away from the guards. Liam fell and rose and fell again, weakening with every step. Just as I heard the sound of boots starting toward us once more, someone pulled us into a tiny alley that branched off the street. The alley was curved and twisted, so narrow that the upper stories of the houses on each side nearly met overhead.

"Here!" cried the man who had plucked us away. "Duck in here!" He led us through a doorway into one of the houses. Gasping and shivering, Liam and I huddled in the entryway, and the man silently urged us into the main room.

Like the house itself, the room was narrow and high, and a fire blazed in a stone hearth at the far end. A tall, gray-haired woman stood there. She motioned us to stand before the flames and warm ourselves. Placing a finger over her lips, she warned us to be still, and we nodded.

We heard the sound of the guards' jangling swords outside, but they passed by the house, following the crowd who had helped us. A moment later, all was quiet.

"Take these," the woman whispered, handing us two rough blankets. We were both dripping wet; icicles hung from Liam's hair, and his lips were blue. I rubbed my head and then Liam's, trying to warm him. He was racked with shivering, and I wrapped both blankets around him.

The man, whom I now recognized as the cobbler who sometimes appeared at the castle to fashion my shoes, came into the room. In a low voice, he said, "You must stay until the guards have searched the apothecary's shop. Then you can go back there."

"The boy needs tending," the woman said softly.

"It is not safe yet," her husband replied, and she nodded.

I tried to convey my gratitude with my eyes. That these people, whom I did not know, would risk so much to help me—it showed a courage I could hardly imagine. The woman smiled grimly at my expression and said, "Our hearts are with you, Princess!"

We sat as close to the fire as we could without scorching ourselves, until the cobbler came back to tell us the guards had left the town. Then we followed him through a rabbit warren of alleys, emerging on the high street just a few shops down from the apothecary's. At the shop door I curtsied to our rescuer, knowing no other way to express my thanks, and he flushed with embarrassment and repeated his wife's words: "Our hearts are with you!"

Brigh and Riona pulled open the door at my knock and caught Liam as he collapsed into their arms. Ennis brought Liam upstairs, peeled off his wet clothes, and wrapped him in blankets. Master Declan said, "Goodness gracious!" over and over again, shaking his head hard enough to make his jowls quiver, as Madame Eveleen heated water and poured it into a copper tub. Brigh pushed Riona, Davina, and me from the room as Liam climbed shivering into the steaming water.

I washed my knees, bloodied from my fall in the market square, and changed into an old overdress of Madame Eveleen's that was far too big for me but dry and warm. We sat on the top stair, Davina clutching Coinin the rabbit, as I told Riona what had happened. She relayed the story to Davina, whose mouth seemed stuck in a little O of astonishment and fear. When Riona, her voice trembling, got to the part about Liam beneath the ice, Davina's eyes opened as wide as her mouth, and she exclaimed, "Goodness gracious!" in a tone so like her father's that I almost wanted to smile. But when the story was done, I said miserably to Riona, *I am sorry. I bring you nothing but danger and hurt.*

We should not have gone.

Riona pursed her lips and did not reply, and I began to feel anxious. I could not bear it if Riona was angry at me.

At least, I added, almost begging, *the swans know now how to break up the ice and keep the water open. They will not have to fly away.* But still she ignored me.

Ennis came from the room, his face troubled. "He has stopped shivering," he told Riona, a gentle hand on her shoulder.

"The guards came here," Davina informed me. "One of them had an enormous mustache that made me want to laugh. They stomped around and made a great deal of noise, and they frightened the poor stoat half to death. But not me—I was not afraid at all! And then they went off, and they stopped at the cooper's, and at the blacksmith's. I think they went everywhere in the whole town!"

And they would return, I knew. How much time did I have before they found me?

"Children!" Brigh called to us. "You can come back in."

Riona helped Davina up, for the girl's arms were full of rabbit, and I stood and followed them in. Warmed by his bath, Liam sat cocooned in blankets in a chair by the fire, sipping a tisane his mother had brewed. The thrush chirped cheerily on his shoulder. I sat beside him with my sewing and apologized again. Indeed, I was getting quite good at asking forgiveness. It seemed I had done little else for days.

"There's no harm done," Liam assured me, but his eyes were bleary and he gave a worrisome cough.

No harm, unless someone who saw us spreads the tale, I pointed out.

In a nearby rocking chair, Brigh shook her head. "It appears that the townspeople do not want to help the queen," she noted.

It seems not, I agreed, recalling how the people in the market had cheered me on and come to our rescue.

"Nevertheless," Brigh said, "we daren't put Master Declan and his family in danger. I think that we—"

"Nonsense!" Master Declan interrupted her. "I said you could stay, and stay you will! We'll have no more of that talk—now I must open the shop." And that, it appeared, was that.

I jumped each time the bell on the door downstairs tinkled, but it was always just a customer. We heard patients talking about the guards; one had seen them returning to the castle. By evening, as I finished my third shirt, I felt I could relax a little.

But it was not to be. Liam had slept uneasily through

most of the afternoon in Ennis's bed, and by night-fall he was flushed and feverish. The cold had gone to his lungs, and he was racked with painful coughing. Brigh, Riona, and Master Declan were up and down the steps with licorice tea; tinctures of hyssop, ground ivy, and chives; and mustard plasters for Liam's chest. I brought my sewing to his bedside so I could watch over him.

As the hours passed, his fever rose, and he began to mutter wildly to himself. I heard words about a lady with green hair, and he sang a snatch of the song the merrow had sung: "'Upon the brimming water among the stones / Are five once-human swans.' Upon the brimming water . . . upon the water . . ." Suddenly he sat bolt upright in the bed, flailing wildly and throwing his blankets to the floor.

"Trapped!" he cried out hoarsely. "I am caught beneath the ice! Oh, help me—I cannot breathe!" We tried to hold him down, to soothe him and quiet him. Then all at once he sank back onto the mattress, insensible.

Pale with worry, Brigh and Riona brought damp cloths, and I abandoned my stitching to cool Liam's hot face. We did not stop ministering to him all night, and all the next day and night as well. I got almost no sewing done as I held his burning hand and tried to calm him when his fever dreams made him believe he was once again trapped below the ice.

At dawn on the third day there came a change. As we watched anxiously, the flush left Liam's face, and he stopped tossing and turning. A sweat broke out on his brow, and when I felt his forehead, he seemed almost cold to my touch. I stepped back. *No. Oh no*, I thought, a terrible fear rising in me. Seeing my expression, Brigh bent over her son and touched his face.

"Oh, children," she said softly. "His fever has broken. He will heal!"

I sagged with relief. Even if I could have spoken, there were no words for what I felt.

"He is sleeping now," Brigh whispered. "And we should as well. I will stay here. You two should rest downstairs."

As we made our way down the stairs in the pale light of dawn, Riona would not meet my eyes. She turned away from me as we tried to make ourselves comfortable on our pallets. I did not know what to do to make her less angry with me, and I was fearful of what she might say, and how much I might deserve her wrath.

The sun was high in the sky and the snow half melted when I woke. Liam was awake upstairs, sipping broth, much improved though still coughing occasionally. But when he saw me, he grinned and said hoarsely, "Why

Princess, I'm beginning to think that it is dangerous to spend time with you!"

I was so glad to see him better that I teased him back, silently retorting, *Well, sir, if a little dunking is too much for you, perhaps a tamer companion would suit you better.*

He laughed, and I was pleased to see color come to his cheeks. "No," he told me, "you are a fine companion for me. I just need a rest from the excitement every now and then."

We spent the day like that, joking back and forth as I stitched away. Davina played at the foot of the bed with Coinin and the stoat, and Brigh bustled in and out of the room, bringing herbal infusions and teas and broth. Riona came as well, but she would not look at me. Finally I could bear the strain between us no longer. I folded my work and said to Liam, *I must stretch my legs for a moment.*

"Bring me a honey cake!" he begged.

You are a very demanding patient, I said, smiling, *but I will do my best.*

I found Riona in the main room, looking out the window at the street life below. I touched her on the shoulder.

"What is it, Meriel?" she asked without turning.

Please talk to me, I began. *I know you blame me for your brother's illness, and I hope you know I did not mean to—*

"Of course you did not mean to!" Riona cried, spinning around. "You never mean to! You just go along doing what you please, not caring who is hurt by it!"

No, that's not true, I protested weakly. *I care—I care terribly. I would give anything to change things, to have kept Liam well. I only thought—*

"But you don't think," Riona interrupted. "You ran off to the lake without a thought for anyone else. What if Liam had drowned? And what of Master Declan and his family, who risk their own lives to help you? You have brought the guards here, and now the whole town is endangered."

A part of me wanted to object, to say *That is not fair! I didn't cause the lake to freeze or your house to burn! I was only trying to help my brothers!* But a small, wiser part knew that there was truth in what Riona said.

You are right, I said at last, miserably. *I never should have gone. I was thoughtless, and I was wrong.*

Riona's expression softened, and she took my hands. "I know you didn't mean to harm Liam," she said gently. "And I'm sorry I was so angry. I should have thought more too—thought of you." I looked at her questioningly. "Now, you see," she explained, "I know better how you feel, for I too have almost lost a brother." I squeezed her hands, my eyes bright with tears, and we smiled at each other.

"You should go back to your sewing," she advised, giving me a brief, awkward hug.

And I won't go out again until it is done! I vowed. Back I went into Ennis's room, now Liam's, only to be met by an expression on Liam's face as cross and disappointed as Riona's had been. He too, it seemed, was harboring anger against me. I squared my shoulders, ready for another accusation, another abject apology.

"Well, where is my honey cake?" he demanded, and I covered my mouth to keep the relieved laughter in as I hurried out to get the cake.

Four shirts were finished by sundown. Shirt four was admirably well sewn—its seams straight, its stitches small and even, its fabric free of blood from my poor pierced fingertips. I walked about the rooms for a few minutes and drank some of Madame Eveleen's good leek soup before starting on the fifth and last.

As I passed the stairway, I heard the shop door open. It was late for a customer, so I glanced down to see who had entered. An old woman, wizened and bent, stood at the long wooden counter, and I saw Master Declan turn to serve her. She had a gray braid that peeped out from beneath the hood of her cloak, and as she placed a wrinkled, ropy hand on the wooden counter, I drew in a startled breath. On that ancient hand was a ruby ring—Lady Orianna's ring. Some might have thought the stone colored glass, but I knew that blood-red jewel. My stepmother the queen was inside the apothecary's shop.

I turned from the stairs in a panic and ran to where Madame Eveleen and Brigh sat before the fire, talking and knitting.

Brigh! I cried silently. *The queen is here!* Catkin, who lay curled beside her owner, rose and hissed. The hair on her back stood straight up.

Immediately Brigh was on her feet. "What is it?" Madame Eveleen asked, frightened at the dismay on our faces.

"The queen is in the shop," Brigh replied, low. "Where are the children?"

"Davina and Ennis have gone out to buy bread before the bakeshop closes," Madame Eveleen said. "And Riona—"

"I am here," Riona whispered, coming in from the kitchen. "What shall we do? Liam cannot be moved!"

"I'll go down," Madame Eveleen told us, heaving her bulk from the rocking chair. "Stay here—and stay quiet!"

"Beware," Brigh said to the apothecary's wife, relaying what I told her, "for the queen does not look like herself, but like an old woman." Madame Eveleen nodded and descended to the shop.

We positioned ourselves at the top of the stairs, where we could not be seen from below, and listened. "Good evening, Mistress," we heard Madame Eveleen say as she reached the foot of the stairs. "What can we do for you?"

"Good evening, Madame Apothecary," the queen said in a voice that both was and was not her own. Anyone who did not know better would think an old woman was speaking, but I could make out Lady Orianna's silky tone beneath the quavering words. "The snow has ended and the sun has melted it away. Still, the cold has left me with a terrible ache in my shoulder. Have you a poultice or an ointment that will soothe the pain?"

"Indeed we do!" said Madame Eveleen cheerily. "My husband will mix monkshood and juniper with boiled white willow skin to make a poultice. You must apply it every evening and morning. In a week or less the pain will disappear."

"Like magic!" the queen marveled. "Are you sure there is no witchcraft in your preparations?" I exchanged a look with Riona. Was the queen trying to learn if she or Brigh was working with the apothecary?

"Oh no," Master Declan said, confused. It was clear

he had no idea who she was. "We use no witchcraft at all, just simple herbology."

Lady Orianna tried a different approach then. "While I wait, perhaps you can tell me about a very strange tale I have heard. A girl and boy were seen as wet as water rats—fallen through the ice while skating, I believe?"

Madame Eveleen laughed, though it sounded strained to me. "Yes, we saw them as they came past the shop, poor things! Did we not hear that they were strangers, Husband, visiting a relative?"

"Ah," said the queen. "And who might that be? There cannot be many strangers here in Tiramore."

Master Declan took his time answering, and I pictured him grinding herbs with his mortar and pestle as he thought. "We did not hear more of the story," he said at last. "Foolish children, not to realize that new ice will not hold!" His careful response made me think that he had become suspicious of the identity of his customer. Perhaps his wife had given him a look or a sign to beware.

"You do not know them, then?" asked the queen, her tone sharper now and more cunning.

"I don't believe so," Master Declan replied. "They were so bedraggled when they passed, though, that I could not have known if they were our next-door neighbors!"

"Though our next-door neighbors' children are but infants," Mistress Eveleen added quickly, not wanting to turn the queen's attention to her neighbors.

"I see," the queen said smoothly, and I suddenly feared that she *did* see. I had the strange, uneasy feeling that her thoughts were spiraling their way up the stairs, searching for me. I backed slowly away, trying to keep my footsteps silent.

"Finished!" I heard Master Declan say in a tone of great relief. "Your poultice is ready, Mistress. Rub it in well, and cover the shoulder with a wool cloth to keep in the healing warmth."

"I thank you, Master Apothecary," said the queen, her voice deceptively humble. "I am greatly impressed with your skill and knowledge. I am sure I will be back soon—very soon! This old body has aches and pains almost daily."

"We should be very glad of your patronage, Mistress," Master Declan said graciously.

We heard the sound of coppers being exchanged, and then the jingle of the bell as the door opened and closed behind Lady Orianna. I sped to the window and watched the queen hobble down the high street in the dusk, her stooped form convincingly old and frail. As she reached the town gate, she turned suddenly, standing straight and tall and looking back at the shop. I ducked quickly, hoping that she had not seen me. I could almost feel the terrible heat of her gaze burn through the windowpane as I dropped to my knees, trembling with fear.

12

The Witch:
And What She Wanted

The sound of the shop door opening below, and Davina's chirpy voice as she came in with her brother, brought me to my feet. I ran into Liam's room. Riona was already perched on the bed, describing to him what had happened.

The queen knows we are here, doesn't she? I asked, but Riona did not have to answer. *I must finish the last shirt!* I said in silent panic. *We haven't much time!*

I picked up my sewing and began to work furiously, my hasty stitches once again long and uneven. There was still so much to do: the shirt front had to be sewn to the back, the sleeves stitched together, and then the finished sleeves attached to the body. Each one of the four shirts I'd completed had taken a full day or more. Who knew how long I had before the queen returned? My desperation unnerved me so much that I sewed the body of the shirt closed, leaving no way to put one's head through. I had to rip the stitches out, my hands trembling.

Liam tried to rise from his bed, but Riona and Brigh urged him to rest.

"You may need your strength before long, lad," Brigh told him somberly, and he lay back, frustrated with his weakness.

"I am so useless!" he fumed. "Meriel, how can I help you?"

Tell me a story to distract me, I suggested, and willingly he complied, as Riona and Ennis stood at the window, watching for the queen or her guards. He told me the tale of Sadhbh, a girl who, because of an enchantment, had to take the form of a deer.

"When the great warrior Finn was out hunting, his dogs ran a deer to ground, and when he came up to them, he found the hounds lying with their heads on the flank of the deer," Liam told us. "Amazed, Finn took the deer home, and in the night it turned into a woman—the beautiful, pearl-pale Sadhbh."

"Oh," breathed Riona, turning momentarily from the window, "did they fall in love?" I looked up briefly, and saw Ennis turn sorrowful eyes on her.

"They did," Liam said, "and they were married. But Finn had to go away to war, and when he came back, Sadhbh had disappeared. Finn searched for her for seven years. He walked the entire land, singing:

> *"'I will find out where she has gone,*
> *And kiss her lips and take her hands;*
> *And walk among long dappled grass,*
> *And pluck till time and times are done*
> *The silver apples of the moon,*
> *The golden apples of the sun.'"*

We were silent for a moment at the beauty and sadness of Finn's song. Then I asked, *Did he find her?*

"Never," said Liam sorrowfully.

So his quest was all in vain?

"No, not entirely. He did not find what he was looking for, but he found a boy seven years old—Ossian, his son by Sadhbh. So it was not a failed quest, but a changed one."

I sewed and sewed as he spoke. Night came and went; the sun passed overhead; shadows grew short across the room and then lengthened again. The front and back of the shirt were attached at last by late afternoon, and I started on the sleeves. I did not stop to eat or stretch my tired limbs. Every now and then Riona would rub my back, or Liam would massage my aching fingers.

Below us the business of the shop went on. Ennis reported to us each time the door opened and the bell jangled, for he could see that we were tense with worry. But the customers were the blacksmith with a burned finger, and the fishmonger's wife with a headache, and a trader passing through with blisters on his feet. None was the queen.

As evening drew nigh, the door sounded one last time, and then we heard the sound of footsteps on the stairs. Ennis came into the room, pushing his blond hair back from his eyes.

"Your Highness," he said to me, "a woman is below, asking to see you."

"An old woman?" Liam said, sitting up. "Is it the queen, disguised?"

"If it is, she is in a different disguise. This lady is not at all old, and she is tall and straight. Her forehead is very high."

Mistress Tuileach! I cried, jumping up. My cloth and needle fell to the floor. I ran from the room, but at the top of the stairs I suddenly remembered Riona's words, harsh but true: *You do not think!* I stopped in my tracks and thought hard. What if it was not my governess? What better way for Lady Orianna to trap me than by pretending to be Mistress Tuileach?

I turned to Riona, who had come up behind me, and said to her, *Have Ennis ask the lady this: What was the last thing she told me before we parted?*

Riona conveyed my request, and Ennis hurried down the stairs. A moment later he was back. "The lady told you, *your love for your brothers is your greatest power,*" he said. I closed my eyes, picturing Mistress Tuileach saying those words, and I clapped my hands with joy.

It is she! It must be—the queen could not have known that! But I was still uncertain, and I looked at Riona and said. *Do you think that it is safe?*

"I believe that it is," Riona replied. "Go and greet her, Meriel!"

I clattered down the stairs, and there, by the great wooden counter, was my beloved governess. She held out her arms, and I flew into them.

Oh Mistress Tuileach, I have missed you so! I exclaimed.

"Now, Princess, it has not been so very long," she said calmly, but her arms were tight around me. "Though I understand that much has happened since we parted."

So much! I cried. *Riona and Liam's house burned—and Liam fell through the ice and was terribly ill—but before that, we saw my brothers in human form! And then—*

"Oh, child, wait, wait," Mistress Tuileach said, smiling at my wild recital. "Let me at least put down my valise and warm my hands."

"Please, Mistress," inserted Madame Eveleen, coming out from behind the counter. "Do come upstairs. We have a fine fire and tea and cakes with which to break your journey. And we would be honored if you would bide with us tonight."

I could not imagine where we would put Mistress Tuileach, for the little rooms were already bursting with guests, but she accepted with gracious relief and mounted the stairs with me. Below, Master Declan closed up the shop, and then he and his wife joined us. Even Liam got out of bed, his color much better and his strength returning. We sat before the crackling fire, and I sewed as Mistress Tuileach revived herself with ginger tea and scones and listened to our tale.

When all had been told, and Mistress Tuileach's hunger and thirst slaked, I asked her, *How did you find us here?*

"When I met Madame Brigh on the road—before the cottage was burned—she and I spoke of her work and how she often consulted with the apothecary. It was all I had to go on, so I thought I would ask here first. A lucky meeting indeed!"

I am so very glad you have come, Mistress Tuileach, I said gratefully.

"I had heard about the fire, even as far away as Corbrack, and I came right away," she said, patting my hand. "I thought you would need all the help you can get. I cannot do much, but I can add my strength to yours, Madame Brigh."

Brigh nodded and said, "The queen is very powerful. And she is a shape-shifter as well. She came into the shop yesterday as an old woman, and only her words—and her ring—gave her away."

Mistress Tuileach put a comforting hand on my shoulder. "Poor child, to have such wickedness set against you!"

I can do the task, I said stubbornly, not looking up as I stitched away.

"I've no doubt that you can. And see how nicely you sew now!" There was great amusement in her voice. "It took only a witch and a terrible enchantment to teach you." I made a sour face at her, but she knew I didn't mean it, and she gave me her rare, transforming smile.

Worn out from her long journey, Mistress Tuileach

slept in Davina's bed that night. Riona and Brigh stayed up to keep me company as I worked, and Davina dozed at my feet until her mother carried her off to sleep in her parents' room. I was determined to finish, but the long hours at Liam's bedside had taken their toll. Riona and Brigh fell dead asleep as they sat, and when all but the last sleeve was sewn, I drifted off despite my best intentions.

The shop-door bell woke me with a start as the first customer of the day entered below. I cursed myself for falling asleep. I stretched my stiff neck and turned back to my endless sewing. Riona and Brigh still slumbered in their chairs, and I let them sleep. Mistress Tuileach brought me tea and bread and butter, and I began to stitch on.

As I threaded my needle, though, I noticed that Catkin was acting oddly. She stalked across the floor, the hair on her back standing straight up. As she walked, she hissed. It was just what she had done the other day, when the queen had come in.

Oh no, I said mutely.

"What is it?" Mistress Tuileach asked, alert at once. Riona and Brigh woke at the sound of her voice.

The cat—look at her. She behaved this way when the queen was here before. I fear she is close again.

"We must remain quiet then," said Mistress Tuileach,

"and guard your thoughts well, child."

I tiptoed to the top of the stairs to listen. Master Declan was helping a customer who needed a remedy for a stomachache, and Madame Eveleen waited on a mother whose child had developed a rash. I could tell there was someone else there, for I could hear footsteps as someone paced around the shop. As the person approached the stairs, Catkin arched her back and hissed, and I shuddered. As the steps faded and moved away, the cat relaxed a bit, but her hair still stood on end. Catkin looked at me, and I saw my own knowledge reflected in her amber eyes: it was the queen who walked below.

Then I heard the shop door open, and Davina's high, fluty voice floated up to me. "Papa!" she cried. "We are back, and we have bought ever so much. Do you know, in the shops everyone was talking about Liam and Princess Meriel, and how they ran from the guards? Only they did not tell where the princess was, and I didn't tell either. I was *so* quiet, wasn't I, Ennis?"

There was a terrible silence that seemed to go on and on. Then the queen spoke in her quavering, old lady voice. "And where is the princess, little girl?"

"Why, she is . . . ," Davina began, but her voice trailed off. It was clear that she had remembered she was not supposed to talk about me. "I do not know where," she improvised. "I could not imagine. I don't know anything about the princess myself, you know. I have never even met her."

I groaned silently.

"Davina!" Madame Eveleen commanded. "Go upstairs with your brother this minute. Can't you see that we have customers?"

"Yes, Mama," Davina said meekly. "Sorry, Mama!" She came running up the stairs, her arms full of packages, and stumbled into my arms, weeping with dismay and fear. Ennis was just behind her. I put my finger across Davina's lips, telling her to stay quiet, and we listened to the conversation downstairs.

"So you are back, Mistress, as you promised," Master Declan said to the queen with false jollity.

"I am, Master," the queen replied.

"And what can I do for you today?"

"I am looking for something very particular," said the queen.

"What is that, Mistress?" Master Declan inquired, his tone cautious now.

"It is not a *what*, but a *who*," the queen said.

"A who? I am sorry, Mistress, but I don't understand you." At the top of the stairs, Brigh and Riona pressed against me as if to share their strength, and the others crowded around.

"I think you do understand me, Master Apothecary," the queen said, and all at once her voice was smooth and imperious, her real voice. "I think there is a girl upstairs who belongs to me."

I gasped. *I have to get out,* I said in desperation to Riona. But this was a mistake. The queen heard my thoughts from the shop below, and she laughed.

"No, you will not get out, Princess," she called. "Come down to me now."

Wide eyed, I looked at Riona, but she did not speak.

"You cannot go to her," Ennis whispered, and Liam said, "I will not let you go to her!" But I realized that days ago Riona had told me what I needed to hear: *And what of Master Declan and his family, who risk their own lives to help you?* I could not put these good people in more danger by refusing to obey.

I must, I said silently to Liam. *And you must stay here, and keep the others up here as well. I am the one she wants. You will all be safe if I go down.*

"No, Meriel!" Liam protested, but he looked at Davina and Ennis and knew that I was right.

Quickly I gathered my sewn shirts together, the last one still unfinished. Liam tried to wrestle the pile from me, but I pulled it back, my mouth set grimly. Riona found a little sack for me, and I stuffed the shirts in. I did not look at anyone—not Mistress Tuileach, nor Brigh, Riona, Liam, Ennis, or Davina, who still hiccuped with tears—as I started down the stairs. My bundle of sewing was hidden in my skirts, and my heart was fluttering in my chest like the thrush with its broken wing. And then I was in the shop, and the queen stood before me, shape-shifted back into the lady Orianna I knew and loathed in all her fearsome beauty.

13

The Battle:
And What Burst Forth

Standing before the queen, somehow I felt my fear fade away. There was only anger in its place—anger that she had taken my father and my brothers from me, anger that she had harmed my friends and destroyed their home. A wonderful strength coursed through me, and I stood very tall and straight and waited for her to speak. Behind the counter, the apothecary and his wife watched us with worried faces. The other customers swiftly completed their purchases and departed, looking nervously behind them as the door closed.

The queen gazed at me and said, "So, Princess, I have found you at last."

I stared back, defiant.

Her dark eyes narrowed. "Did you think you could hide from me? I sensed you when I was here before. I only needed to be certain."

And here I am, I taunted her. *What will you do with me?*

She pursed her lips. "Well, that is the question, isn't it? I had underestimated you. I did not think you would stand in my way, once your brothers were gone."

You were quite mistaken, I pointed out. *In fact, you have been very sloppy. Did you not see that my father had five sons when you married him? Surely you could have chosen a childless king to enchant and torment, and saved yourself the trouble of eliminating us. It would have been far easier to set your plan in motion with another man.*

She scowled. "You alone were in his thoughts when I met him. A daughter did not matter to me, for you could never rule his kingdom. He did not think of your brothers, and I did not ask if he had other children. You are quite right—it was my mistake indeed. But I will not make another."

It pleased me greatly that I had been uppermost in Father's mind, but I concealed this thought. Instead I said, *Father will soon see you for what you really are. Then he will be done with you, and you will be vanquished. You will never open the door to Faerie.*

She laughed. "I think you underestimate *me*, my dear. The door is already opening. And your father is mine, well and truly. Whether he is under a spell or not, he will stay with me."

I did not believe her. I knew that Father could never truly love her, not if he knew what she had done.

"And what is that in your bag, little Meriel?" the queen asked me in a cunning voice, moving toward me.

It is nothing, I said, stepping back.

"Nothing? Nothing spun from nettles, woven and sewn? I know what you have been doing, you silly girl. Give it to me," she demanded.

I clutched the sack to me and shook my head. How I wanted to shout at her, to tell her that I never would obey her!

"Give it to me," she repeated, and again I refused. Her eyes flashed with anger, and the fear that I thought I had conquered returned in full force. I could feel the pull of her power, coiling around me as the tendrils of fog had when the merrow appeared at Heart Lake. I fought to stay still, not to go to her, not to hand her the shirts as she insisted.

As I silently resisted, her fury grew wilder, until it was too much for her to contain. Suddenly a jar on the lowest shelf behind the counter exploded, sending shards of blue and white porcelain flying through the shop. I ducked as the sweet smell of anise filled the air. Madame Eveleen, frozen behind the counter with Master Declan, shrieked in terror as another jar exploded, and then another. Flying pieces of earthenware careened through the air, and odors of herbs and tinctures filled the shop. Master Declan pulled his wife from behind the counter, and they fled to the examination room as the glass flasks broke open and then the large jars on the upper shelves burst, spilling their dreadful contents. Colored liquids cascaded down the shelves, red and yellow and purple and blue mixing together to form a putrid brownish waterfall. The air was thick and noxious with fumes; I could barely see the queen as she stood amid the swirling gases.

I felt someone grab my arm, pulling me toward the front door. It was Liam. I took his hand and followed him, ducking below the foul vapors. When we reached the door, I tried to pull it open, but as my hand touched the knob, a blast of wind blew through the shop, pushing against the door. I pulled as hard as I could, but the wind was stronger.

I cannot open it! I cried to Liam. He could not help me; he was overcome with coughing from the fumes, his lungs still weak from his illness.

"You must!" he gasped between coughs.

I pulled and pulled, but it was no use. I was not

strong enough. I sagged in defeat, and I heard the queen begin to laugh.

Then I thought of my brothers, paddling helplessly on the freezing lake, and my love for them surged through me. *Cullan!* I cried silently. *Darrock! Aidan, Baird, Druce! I am coming!* I pictured them in my mind as I had last seen them in their human form, their beloved faces and familiar smiles, the way they stood and moved and spoke and teased. I heaved on the door with all my might, and it creaked open just enough for Liam and me to slip through.

Out on the street we took great gulps of untainted air, and Liam's coughs slowed and stopped. Then we began to run toward the lake. We passed clusters of townspeople, bewildered and amazed as they tried to see what was happening inside the apothecary's shop, but the interior was utterly obscured by the billowing vapors even as the crash and shattering of glass and pottery continued.

We ran so fast that I could not have spoken aloud, but silently I asked Liam, *I haven't finished the last shirt. What shall I do?* But he had no breath to spare and only shook his head.

At last we reached the lake. There was no sign of my brothers. We stood on the shore panting, our breath pluming in the frosty air, and tried to see if they were along the banks or hidden in the weeds. But there was nothing. All the other birds had gone; the reeds and grasses were bent and brown, wilted in the cold. It seemed that nothing at all lived there.

Oh no, I thought despairingly. *Where could they be? There is still open water; surely they have not flown off.*

"They must be at the other end," Liam pronounced.

But they know the danger! We've told them not to go! I protested.

"Perhaps they had no choice. Perhaps they were summoned."

I was about to ask, *Summoned by whom?* But I realized that I did not want to know the answer. Instead I began to slog around the lake, slipping on icy mud and clambering over rocks. I kept my bag clutched tightly in one hand, though it unbalanced me. I knew that the shirts I had sewn were my brothers' only chance.

We hurried through the mist, and then it cleared as it had twice before, and we could see the spring from Faerie. There was no merrow there, nor any other horrific visitor from below, and my brothers swam placidly at the spot where the spring met the lake water. At our clumsy approach they turned, and I could see their eyes light up when they saw me. I hadn't visited them in days. They looked thinner beneath their feathers, and I worried that they had been hungry, for the water plants they ate had withered and died. I waved, and they clapped their beaks with pleasure.

And then suddenly came the sound I had feared: the voice of Lady Orianna.

"Did you think to escape me, you foolish girl?" the queen said in a gentle, reproving tone. "Do you not know that I am faster than you, stronger than you, smarter than you?"

Somehow, she had made her way to the lake's end before we did, and she was standing on the same rock where the merrow had sat combing her long green hair. She towered above my brothers, and she was beautiful, her hair dark against her white skin and her black eyes flashing, her full lips drawn downward in a forbidding scowl. The swans did not flee from her; caught by her magic, they were simply treading the water with their webbed feet, staring up at her in mute obedience.

Her quiet voice was more frightening to me than her wrath in the apothecary's shop had been. It was clear that she felt no threat from me, even though she knew I held the shirts that could break her spell. I trembled before her, but I swore I would not show my fear. Instead I summoned all my own anger as I had in the shop, drew together all the spoiled rages and tantrums I had inflicted on family and servants over the years, and turned it on her.

You evil creature, I cried fiercely, *how dare you force your way into my family and hurt us? Do you believe we can't see you for what you really are? You are older than dust, and your wickedness shows in the creases of your aged face!*

Without thinking, she brought a hand to her cheek as if to touch the wrinkles I had described. I smiled grimly. I had made her doubt her own disguise!

But a moment later she smiled too. "Ah, Meriel," she sighed, "you cannot best me. Your pouting is a tiny pinprick, no more. If you yield now, and hand me the shirts, I shall do as I promised—send you to school and then marry you off to a man who will tame you. You will not be harmed."

I looked at my swan brothers, their snow-white feathers and long arched necks, and in a fury shouted silently, *No! I shall never give up!*

She laughed then. "Child, child," she said serenely. "I shall sweep you aside as if you were an insect."

Insects bite and sting! I goaded her.

"Your sting will not harm me," she replied.

"Ah, but our stings might," said a voice behind me. I spun around. There, close together, were Mistress Tuileach, Brigh, and Riona. Surely we would be more powerful together than the lady Orianna alone!

"No, Princess," Lady Orianna retorted, as if I had spoken aloud. She ignored the others completely. "You do not begin to match me in power. Now, give me the shirts." Her gaze was cold on me, and I shivered again. As hard as I struggled, I could not control my feet as they began a slow, stumbling march toward her. Liam reached out to hold me back, and behind me I could hear Brigh call out something, but I could not stop. I tried to summon my wrath again, but it seemed a petty, meager thing against such a force.

Then I thought of how I had found the strength to pull open the shop door, and I realized that anger could not vanquish a creature such as Lady Orianna. I recalled the terms of the spell the queen had cast. *If the seamstress speaks before the task is done, each word will be as a knife in the victims' hearts.* Before the task is done—but I had finished, or nearly finished. I had done as much as I could.

And so I found my voice again, the voice I had not used in all those long days. I put all the love I had into my words as I croaked, "Brothers! Come to me!" Then I squeezed my eyes shut, afraid that I had killed them all by speaking aloud.

But when I looked again, they were still there, alive and turned toward me, their feet paddling furiously. The current from Faerie flowed stronger now, pushing them away, and they fought against it.

"Darrock!" I screamed. "Come to me!" The biggest swan broke free of the current and swam as fast as he could until he was before me. I fumbled in my sack for the largest shirt and swiftly threw it over his swan head. The queen let out a cry of rage as the shirt settled on him and he began to change, just as he had on the night of the full moon. From head to foot his swan features—beak and neck, wings and webbed feet—transformed until he stood, a man again, in the water in front of me. He looked dazed, holding out his hands to see if fingers graced them, peering over his shoulder to look for his swan tail feathers.

I had no time to greet him. "Cullan! Baird!" I cried.

"Hurry, Meriel," Riona begged. I looked briefly at her and could see a terrible strain on her face. Beside her I saw Brigh and Mistress Tuileach, their hands moving in arcs, their voices speaking strange words designed to keep the queen from me. As I watched, first Riona, then Mistress Tuileach were forced to their knees by the power of the queen's witchcraft. Only Brigh remained standing, and I could see that she was weakening.

And then, without warning, there was a great hue and cry from the direction of the town. I turned to see the people of Tiramore, led by Ennis, running toward the lake. I could recognize the cobbler and his wife, the blacksmith, the baker, and the cooper. Everyone I had met and seen, and many more I did not know, had left the safety of home and hearth to aid me.

The shock of their appearance startled the queen, diverting her strength. Riona and Mistress Tuileach rose to their feet again, and I swiftly pulled two more shirts from my sack as Baird broke free of the current and hurried to me. The Cullan swan, though, held back and pushed Druce toward me. In a moment I had thrown the shirts over Baird and Druce, and two more brothers stood before me, restored and blinking with amazement.

The queen, enraged beyond all measure now, called out something in an unknown language. To my horror, I saw that with her words the current from Faerie, which had been flowing into the lake, had abruptly reversed itself. Now it ran back into the crevice in the earth, and the two remaining swans, Aidan and Cullan, were pulled along with it.

"Cullan! Aidan!" I screamed. "Come to me! Come to me!" They paddled wildly, but the current was stronger than they were and drew them closer and closer to the dread opening that led to the lands below.

"Ennis, help them!" Riona cried desperately. I turned and saw Ennis, his face a map of terrible conflict. He looked at Riona, his feelings for her clear in his expression. Then he looked at the swans, and I knew what he was thinking. If he helped them, if he saved Cullan, he would lose Riona. If he did not . . .

There was a splash, and Ennis plunged into the lake up to his knees. He waded through the freezing water toward the swans as the birds flapped their huge wings, trying to escape the pull of the current. Ennis was submerged up to his neck by the time he reached the swans, and I could see his lips turning blue with the cold. He reached out one arm to grab Aidan, then the other to hold Cullan. But he too was pulled by the Faerie stream, and his strength waned rapidly in the icy surge.

As the other townspeople urged them on, the black-smith and the cobbler ran into the lake, reaching for Ennis. Without thinking, I too leaped into the water, breathless with the shock of it. I held the last two shirts high over my head as I struggled toward my brothers. I could hear the queen howling in rage behind me. The lake seemed to hold me back, but I labored on until I was in the Faerie current. And then I was pulled toward the chasm as my feet left the lake bottom, for the water was over my head.

As I floated past, Cullan, still in Ennis's grasp, opened his great wing and caught me. I clung to him with one hand as with the other I tried to throw a shirt over his head, but he ducked and the shirt landed on Aidan. Aidan stuck his beak through the neckhole at the top, and the shirt settled over him. In a moment he was my brother again, splashing and gasping in Ennis's arms.

Now we were at the very edge of the chasm, and the water passed through it and down, a relentless waterfall to the lands below. I could see the lights and hear the music from Faerie over the rumble of the cataract. My face, the only part of me above water, was bathed in a warm breeze that came from beneath the earth. I smelled all the scents of spring in that gentle wind, and for an instant I longed to sail over the edge down to whatever waited at the bottom. I saw again the golden throne, the beautiful men and women who stood below, ready to wait on me and obey my every word. My hold on Cullan's wing began to loosen. With a clack of his beak, he bent his long neck and gave me a sharp nip on the cheek, and I cried out in pain, awakened from my momentary dream.

"The last shirt, Meriel!" Liam shouted from the shore, and I held it up, treading water frantically. It was the one-armed shirt, the only one left. I slipped it over Cullan's head, and it drifted down over him. From his head down, my beloved brother emerged from his swan form—but for the wing that I held with all my might, for there was no sleeve to cover that wing, to change it back to a human arm.

At that moment the pull of the current from Faerie

stopped. All movement stopped, and all sound as well. The incantations that Riona, Mistress Tuileach, and Brigh had been chanting ceased, the people of Tiramore quieted. The silence was eerie.

Then, from the crack in the earth, came a great thundering noise that dwarfed the roar the waterfall had made. Panicked, the blacksmith and cobbler grasped Ennis and pulled, and Aidan, Cullan, and I were pulled with him, away from the gap. The sound grew louder and louder, our attempts to escape more and more frantic.

All at once, the crevice exploded with a jet of steaming water, and the torrent spewed out the most ghastly creature I had ever seen or imagined. It was like an enormous eel, but its head was flat and circular and all mouth, with teeth as long as kitchen knives and as sharp as needles. As the waterspout threw the beast upward and I could see that its tail was forked, it twisted its impossibly long body in an airborne dance that was at once graceful and unbearably terrifying. A flicker of flame darted out of the creature's mouth.

"It is an onchu!" Brigh cried. "Oh, children, flee!"

As the onchu plunged into the lake with a great splash and disappeared below the surface, I screamed in fear, and I could hear the people of Tiramore crying out in alarm. Cullan scooped me up with his swan's wing and slung me over his shoulder. We all scrambled desperately for the shore. We were certain that at any moment the beast's vile mouth would close around us and its needle teeth would tear us to pieces.

But we were not what the onchu wanted. As we reached the shore and Cullan placed me back on my feet, we saw the creature surface again from the depths and circle around, moving back toward the place where the Faerie current emerged. Speechless with dread, we watched as the great monster slowly rose up, and up and up, gyrating until only its tail was below the water. Towering above the lake's surface, twisting and writhing, it turned its foul face to the lady Orianna. The creature breathed a tongue of fire at her and then spoke in a loathsome hiss.

"You have not sssucceeded in your quessst. You have broken your promissse. Your sssson will not be king, and the door will clossse again. Your failure makesss you mine. Mine. Mine!"

Lady Orianna gave a shriek of horror and scrabbled backward, forgetting that she stood on a moss-covered rock. Losing her footing, she slid into the Faerie stream. The onchu bent to her, its eel body swaying, and she covered her eyes with her arm. She shrieked again, her lips forming a terrified O that mirrored the onchu's enormous fiery mouth as it opened and closed around her. And then she was gone.

We stood on the water's edge utterly stunned, unable to move or speak. The beast never looked at us or acknowledged our existence in any way. It suddenly dove into the Faerie stream, and we saw its long, twisting body ooze over the edge of the crevice to the lands below. Its forked tail flicked once in the air as it disappeared from sight.

"Oh, look," Cullan whispered, his good arm tight around me. As if following in the wake of the onchu, the Faerie current had reversed again, and it seemed to be pulling the whole lake with it. Wordlessly, the people of Tiramore joined us on the banks. I don't know how long we stood there, shivering with cold and shock, as the water gushed and roared down the chasm. Rocks, logs, plants, everything that had been in the lake surged over the edge and away in a thundering rush. At last it all was gone. Then the crevice in the earth closed, just as a door closes, with a gentle click. All that was left was a muddy, heart-shaped depression in the ground. Heart Lake was no more.

14

The End:
And What Was Celebrated

Somehow we made our way up the hill to the castle, aided by the townspeople. Mistress Tuileach, Brigh, Riona, and Liam were exhausted from their battle with the queen. Still, they were stronger than Aidan, Cullan, Ennis, and I—and the cobbler and blacksmith—who were soaked through and half frozen. As we stumbled up the slope, Darrock lifted me up, as one would carry a baby. I struggled very halfheartedly to escape, but gave up quickly and rested in his arms.

Halfway there, I heard a woman cry out, and I

raised my head from Darrock's chest to see Madame Eveleen, Master Declan, Davina, and Father running toward us. Darrock put me down and I found myself in Father's embrace. Davina threw herself at Ennis, speaking nonstop.

"We thought you were dead, Brother! We ran up to the castle when you left, for the shop was all destroyed and we needed suchor—soaker—such—"

"Succor," Ennis said gently, holding his sister tight.

"We needed help! And the king met us, and he was ever so kind, and then we heard dreadful noises and saw fire on the lake—how could there be fire on water? And then—*whoosh!* The lake was all gone! What happened to it? And we didn't know—we didn't know if you . . ." And she burst into tears, sobbing too hard to continue speaking.

"But you see I am alive and well, Davina," Ennis reassured her. "We all are."

"Your brother was a hero, Davina," Riona said. That stopped her tears immediately.

"Really, a hero?" she said in amazement. "Did he fight with a sword? Did he kill anybody? He was very brave, I am sure, for he has always been brave. But a hero—!"

"He saved my life," Cullan said soberly. "Mine, and Aidan's as well." And he bowed to Ennis, who looked quite taken aback.

Then my father spoke. "Oh, Sons," he said in a voice just above a whisper. "Oh, Daughter. What have I done?" His face was a mask of anguish, and I noticed for the first time the streaks of gray in his brown beard. But his eyes were clear, no longer glassy with enchantment.

I tightened my arms around him. "You did nothing wrong," I said firmly, though my voice was still weak from disuse. "It was she—the lady Orianna. Not you. Never you!"

"Where is she?" he asked me, and I hesitated.

"Your Majesty, the queen is gone for good," Mistress Tuileach told him. Her eyes were full of compassion.

"It is for the best," he said softly. "She was not who I thought. What she did to my children . . ." He shook his head angrily. "I should have been stronger. I should have known."

"Should have, could have, would have," Mistress Tuileach said tartly, surprising us all. "Your Majesty, this is not the time for blame and sorrow. We are all alive and well, as Master Ennis said—and many of us are sopping wet. Let us go inside and dry off. We will catch our deaths standing here in the cold."

Father's expression lost a little of its distress, and he looked at us, one by one, as if counting to make sure we were all there. And then he looked at his subjects, ranged around us, and his face cleared and filled with wonderment.

"Yes, yes, of course!" he exclaimed. "Everyone—Master Quillan, Mistress Mealla, Master Ailin—come inside. Boys, Meriel, everyone, come in, come in." I was amazed. He seemed to know every person there, and I realized he had spent time with them in his weekly audiences over the years and remembered them all. It was no wonder they loved him so, and had risked so much to help me!

"Your Majesty," the cobbler, Master Quillan said, "we shall leave you with your family. We only wanted to be sure all were safe."

Hoarsely, I said, "We are safe because of you, and all your neighbors. We could not have . . ." But my voice gave out, and I could only curtsy, as I had done to the cobbler once before. The townspeople, as one, bowed to us. Then they turned and set off back down the hill to their homes.

We staggered into the castle, past the guards who were now only our own men. The queen's guards had disappeared, never to be seen again. Ogan was there, his lance in hand, and he bowed as we passed. Mistress Tuileach and Brigh helped me up the stairs, dried me off, and clothed me in a warm woolen dress as Davina danced around us, chattering.

"Is the witch gone, then?" she asked me as Mistress Tuileach tried to comb the tangles from my wet curls. I nodded.

"But what happened to her? Did you see what she did to our shop? Oh, Papa was so angry! And Mama cried. Such a terrible mess, I couldn't believe it. Do you know, every single bottle and jar was broken! Every last one! She was very bad, wasn't she?"

I felt much better, snug and dry, and I smiled at Davina's endless stream of questions. "She was very bad indeed," I replied, my voice sounding strange to me. I was so used to thinking my speech that speaking aloud was like an echo in my head, the thought first, and then the spoken words. I formed each word carefully, as if I were blowing bubbles. "But she is gone now, gone for good. And I am sure Father will have your shop rebuilt and all those jars replaced, for it was our fault that it was ruined."

"Goodness gracious, really?" Davina cried. "Oh, I must tell Papa!" And she sped out of my room as I laughed helplessly.

Mistress Tuileach herded everyone into the old nursery, the coziest room in the castle, where there were toys and wonders aplenty for Davina to marvel over. My brothers all were there, and the apothecary's family, and Brigh and Riona and Liam. Cullan sat on the settee, a cloak covering his swan wing, and beside him sat Riona, and next to her was Ennis. They made a rather uncomfortable threesome, I thought, glancing at them. Brigh, Master Declan, and Madame Eveleen sat on the worn old sofa across from them, my other brothers having insisted they take the comfortable seat. The rest of us sprawled on the floor, except for Mistress Tuileach, who sat very upright on a stool.

I settled myself between Aidan and Druce, looking from brother to brother. They all seemed well, though a little thin and drawn. "Aidan," I said, growing more used to speaking with every word, "what was it like to be a swan?"

"Oh, did you fly?" Davina asked, flapping her arms like wings. "I've flown in my dreams, but then I try it when I wake up and I always fall down. Was it wonderful?"

Aidan chuckled. "We did not master flying," he admitted. "Swans are very big—it's not easy to get into the air. I came close, toward the end. Something in us urged us to fly, to go to southern places. I wish I had flown." His face was thoughtful, remembering.

"It was not much fun being a swan," Druce complained. "We had to eat weeds, and the water was cold.

There was nothing much to do but swim. I shall never swim again!"

"And I shall never eat wild greens again," Baird added, making a face that caused Davina to giggle.

"Nor fowl," I said, recalling how the smell of roast chicken now turned my stomach.

When Father entered the room, servants behind him carrying trays of cakes and steaming drinks, everyone but Davina stood.

"No, no," Father said, motioning us to sit. "Please, do not get up. None of you need ever rise in our presence again. I am so indebted to you—though I still do not know quite what has happened."

Father sat on a tufted hassock, and Brigh and Riona told him the whole story, from Riona's first meeting with me to the discovery of my brothers in swan form, from the harvesting and spinning of the nettles to the weaving and sewing of the shirts, from the fire at Brigh's house to our flight to the apothecary's, from the destruction of the shop to the terrible confrontation at the lake.

Father listened, his eyes wide, his brow darkening and furrowing at times with anger or concern. When Brigh described the creature that came up from Faerie and devoured Lady Orianna, he closed his eyes as if in pain. Even Davina was quiet as the tale was told. At its end, Father shook his head in wonder.

"I knew some of it as it occurred," he said. "I could sense that she was . . . wrong, somehow, and that something evil was happening. But it was as if I were watching from behind a pane of old glass, wavy and distorted. I could not see things clearly, no matter how I tried, and I could not reach through to help the ones I loved. I am so very sorry, my children." His voice broke.

Then Darrock spoke. "None of us faults you, Father. We were all under her spell—none of us could resist."

"Except me," I pointed out. I could not help myself.

All the heads in the room swiveled to stare at me, and there was a moment's silence. Then Cullan snorted with laughter, and even Father's lips twitched in a smile.

"Modest as always, Sister!" Cullan observed. I scowled at him.

"But it is true," Darrock stated in his formal way. "Meriel completed tasks none of us guessed she could perform. Without her, all would have been lost." He wriggled a little, a movement that in a bird might have been seen as wagging his tail feathers, and Cullan snorted again.

"Missing your tail, Prince?" he asked, and we all started to laugh. Darrock flushed, his dignity wounded.

"At least I am not still part bird," he pointed out, speaking, as I once did, without thinking. The room fell quiet.

Cullan shrugged off the cloak, exposing his wing. Father, who had not noticed it in the tumult of our reunion, drew in a sharp breath.

"Yes, Brother," Cullan said lightly. "I remain part swan, to remind us of our time enchanted. And a swan wing is not to be taken lightly!" He rose from the settee. "Did you know that a swan can break a man's leg with the strength of its wing?" Casually, Cullan swept his wing across the floor where Darrock sat, and the force of the blow, as gentle as it seemed, sent Darrock sprawling. We all gasped, unsure of his reaction to such disrespect.

Darrock picked himself up deliberately, brushing off his tunic and adjusting it with great decorum. "Well, Cullan," he said at last, "it may be that your wing will make up for your deficiencies with a sword." A joke— from Darrock! I was too surprised to laugh, but Davina giggled, and I saw Druce cover a grin.

"I wish I had a wing!" Davina cried. "I could have knocked over the blacksmith's son when he tormented me, and I could use it to cool myself when it is hot, and I am sure it could fan a fire till it roared!"

I stood and ran over to Cullan. "It is my fault," I

reminded him. "I couldn't finish my task. If only I had sewn faster. . . ." I reached out and touched the soft white feathers.

"You did an exceptional job, Meriel," Cullan assured me. "Look at your hands! Their scars and calluses bear witness to your courage and determination. I am so very proud of you."

When I looked up at him I could see his smile through the tears on my lashes. But his eyes were sorrowful as he turned to Riona. He folded his wing carefully by his side and bowed to her, saying, "My love, you could not have foreseen this . . . this accident of nature when we made our vows these months ago. You should not be yoked to half a man, as I am now. I release you from your promise."

I gaped. Vows? They had plighted their troth, and told no one? My shock was reflected in Brigh's and Liam's expressions, and in Father's. I looked at Ennis and saw a sudden look of hope in his eyes.

Riona rose with a grace that belied her worn dress and wooden shoes. She went to Cullan and touched his folded wing with a gentle hand.

"I have pledged myself to you, my dearest," she said softly. "Your wing does not make you less of a man, but more. And it makes you more like me—as I am part witch, so you are part swan."

Cullan shook his head. "You deserve better," he said simply.

"I want nothing better," Riona replied. "For me, there is nothing better. Your wing will be a reminder to us always of the bonds of love, for do swans not mate for life?"

Cullan breathed a deep sigh of relief, unfolded his wing again, and wrapped it around Riona, hiding their faces from our sight, though we knew that behind the feathers they were kissing. I glanced again at Ennis and saw he had turned away, and my heart ached for him. He had known, when he leaped into the lake, that this would happen. Riona was right: he truly was a hero.

Then Cullan asked Brigh formally for Riona's hand, and presented her to Father, who received her as a daughter with a loving embrace. I hugged her too, saying, "You shall be my sister! At last, I will have someone to defend me against my brutish brothers!"

Riona squeezed me hard and laughed. "But I will have to take Cullan's side when you disagree. You shall have to ask Liam to defend you then."

Liam said, "I don't think Meriel needs defending. In fact, I think it is her brothers, not she, who will need my help!" I swatted at him and he dodged out of the way, his blue eyes dancing.

Master Declan and his family departed when the

cakes were all eaten. The rooms above their shop were still habitable, and Father assured them that he would have the shop rebuilt immediately, replacing the goods the queen had destroyed with plants from the castle's own garden when spring came.

"Riona and I will grow the herbs you need," I promised them. "You will have a supply of whatever you want from us, or from Brigh." For Father had promised to build Brigh a cottage, too, to take the place of her burned home, and this one would be closer to the castle so Brigh could visit whenever she pleased, and Liam could tend the castle animals more easily.

I hugged them all and kissed Davina, who chirped, "May I visit you, Princess? May I come anytime I please? May I play with the toys when I come? Oh, do say yes!" I laughed and said yes, and we sent them home with a servant carrying food and another carrying clothes, and a third, at my direction, bearing a sack filled with dolls and costumes and balls and games of all sorts to keep Davina happy during the cold indoor days to come.

The rest of us drank spiced cider as the heat from the nursery fire made us drowsy. My brothers toasted me with their cups for my bravery, and I beamed and blushed with happiness, leaning against Father's knee.

"How did you have the strength to do it, Daughter?"

he marveled, stroking my hair tenderly.

"It was not my strength alone," I replied. "It was Riona's, and Liam's, and Brigh's, and the strength of the love that all the people of Tiramore bear you." I described again how the townspeople had helped us, how Ogan the guard had come to our aid, how the cobbler and his wife had taken us in, how he and the blacksmith had braved the icy water to pull us to safety. Father vowed to reward them all with treasure and advancement. And then I said, "Truly, though, it was Mistress Tuileach's wisdom that gave me my real power."

"A wise woman indeed," Father said, smiling at my governess. She reddened under his look, and all at once I realized something I had long been too blind to see. How could I not have known before? Why, Father should marry Mistress Tuileach!

Brigh, Riona, Liam, and Mistress Tuileach all turned to look at me, and I realized they had heard my thought. Mistress Tuileach was pink with embarrassment, but Liam grinned and nodded at me. I almost wished I had spoken aloud, for I feared that Mistress Tuileach was too duty bound and too proper, and Father too afraid to seek love again after his experience with Lady Orianna, for such a thing ever to come to pass. But I had learned a little from my weeks of enforced silence, and so I bit my tongue and managed to keep quiet.

Then Father, ignorant of our unspoken conversation, stretched and said, "To bed, all. It is late, and you have earned your rest. And we have a wedding to begin planning in the morning!"

We did indeed have a wedding, not many weeks later. It was to be a quiet ceremony, just Riona's family and mine. Riona and I went to Tiramore to the draper's shop, where we purchased a length of beautiful creamy satin, though Riona protested at first that linen would do well enough for her.

"Linen?" I scoffed. "You will be a princess, and wed in satin. I will allow no argument!" Stroking the smooth cloth, she quickly gave in. Mistress Tuileach designed the gown, and she and I sewed it, my stitches neat and small and even enough to meet with my governess's approval. Mistress Tuileach embroidered the hem and sleeves with the flowers Riona loved, for it was too late in the year for her to carry a bouquet. The dress was simple but beautiful, nipped in at the bride's slender waist and flowing to the floor in graceful folds. Riona was exquisite in it, her dark hair and blue eyes set off by the pale fabric. She marveled at the shoes the cobbler made for her—no wooden shoes these, but soft white satin with tiny curved heels.

Before the ceremony, I took Riona aside. "Will you wear this?" I asked her, holding out the sapphire stone Cullan had given me. I had restrung it on a narrow chain of gold. "It is something old, something borrowed, and something blue, to go with your new gown."

Riona took it from me. "I would be honored," she said in a low voice, gazing at the jewel. "I know you value it greatly, for you have never taken it off as long as I've known you. I will return it after I am wed." I fastened it around her neck, and she embraced me, her face bright with happiness.

When the vows had been said and the couple toasted with sparkling wine, we threw open the heavy door of the forecourt and invited the townspeople in. Braziers heated the space. In the torchlight a small group of musicians from the town played lively dances for the tradespeople and merchants whom I had observed from the rooms above the apothecary's shop, who had urged me on and hidden me and held me up when I most needed it.

Father's old friends Sir Brion and Sir Paidin, Lord Osan and Lord Saran arrived with their wives. Master Declan and his family joined us, and we greeted them with great pleasure. Davina was thrilled to be able to stay up for her first grown-up party, and Ennis came with the tailor's daughter, a pretty, high-spirited girl with dark curls who looked just a little like Riona. I watched them dance as I sat eating cake with Liam.

"So his heart was not completely broken," I observed, smiling as they spun on the smooth cobblestones.

"I'm glad," Liam said, "for he is a good man, and he deserves happiness."

"She is very nice indeed," Davina piped up, hopping around us in her version of the dance. "She has taught me to sew!"

I laughed, thinking of my torturous hours spent over needle and thread. "A fine skill to have," I told her wryly, passing her a thick slice of wedding cake. "But be sure you use linen to make your dresses—stay away from nettles!"

Liam nudged me and pointed. "Look at that!" he said. I looked, and saw that Father was leading Mistress Tuileach in a quadrille. Her face was flushed as much with delight as with the warmth from the braziers, and she looked as pretty as ever she had.

"Do you think . . . ?" I asked, wondering.

"It is not for you to say, Princess, though I'm sure you would like to," Liam teased me. "Only time will tell." I stuck out my tongue at him and he said, "Shall we join them? It looks like they need another couple for the dance." And I put down my cake and whirled off with him across the cobblestones.

There were toasts and more dances. The boys from Tiramore laid a wooden barrel top on the ground and then competed to see who could perform the wildest sean-nós dance atop it, their feet tapping on the wood, their arms waving wildly. Then town couples danced a ceili in a long line as Baird played on his harp and the other guests stood around them in a circle, clapping and calling out the steps. It was a far cry from the formal dance Lady Orianna had hosted, and even from the balls Father had given in years past, but it was the most fun I had ever had. Liam and I joined in the ceili with great abandon, and of course Riona and Cullan danced too, though Cullan was clumsy with his wing and knocked over a dancer or two accidentally.

The newlyweds left for their wedding journey in a white carriage as snow began to fall gently. The party continued in the forecourt, but my brothers, Father, Liam, Brigh, and I stood by the lane and bade the happy couple farewell as they departed. Riona pressed a kiss onto my forehead and whispered, "I will be back before spring, Sister, and then we will plant our garden!" Once in the carriage she leaned out the window to wave good-bye, her smile radiant.

Cullan hugged us, me last of all, and climbed in after her, folding his wing awkwardly as he sat. As the horses began to trot away, he leaned out the other side of the carriage and called to me, but I could not hear him. I picked up my skirts and ran after them, crying, "What? What is it?"

He shouted more loudly, and at last I heard him over the clatter of the horses' hooves: "Behave yourself when I am gone, Meriel!"

His customary parting words brought tears of joy and sadness to my eyes, for all that had changed and all that still remained the same. And as the carriage jangled down the lane, I whispered back, in a voice that only I could hear, "And you too, my dearest brother!"

1

Of Honey and a Haircut

Luna had disappeared again.

I was always amazed at how easily my little sister got away from me. She was my responsibility, and keeping track of her was nearly a full-time job. I had searched the top floors of the palace already and was starting to get worried. If I didn't find her before lunch, Papa would be upset and Mama would be frantic.

I ran down the stone stairs to the kitchen. It was usually deserted at that time of day, but I knew that Luna sometimes crept in when Cook was busy elsewhere and grabbed a leftover slice of cake or bowl of pudding. And my guess was right.

Luna *was* there, but she wasn't eating. Instead, she sat in one of the wooden chairs that lined the long table where the servants took their meals. She was holding out a thick strand of her curly brown hair, pulling so hard it was nearly straight. I realized she had a butter knife in her other hand.

"Luna," I said, "whatever are you doing?"

She turned her head to look at me.

"I'm cutting my hair," she said, lifting the knife.

"Oh no—your pretty curls!" I protested, hurrying around the table to her. "You mustn't!"

"My hair isn't pretty, Aurora," Luna countered. "It's the color of dirt, not blond like yours. And it's always tangled. I am sick to death of it, and I want it gone."

"If you ever used a brush, it wouldn't be tangled," I scolded. "And you can't just chop at it—you'll look dreadful. Ask Madame Claude to show you how to style it." Madame Claude was Mama's hairdresser, skilled at weaving jewels through my hair and piling Mama's fair curls as high as one of Cook's soufflés. But I had to admit that she had never been able to control Luna's wild mane.

Luna scowled. "You know that Madame Claude can't tame my hair with hairpins or combs. If you think I can't cut it well, then you do it!"

At first I shook my head. "Mama won't like it," I warned.

"I don't care. I'll do it alone if you won't help."

If Luna hurt herself, I would be blamed, and Mama would take to her bed in distress. And perhaps if I did as she asked, it wouldn't turn out too badly. I moved behind her, took a handful of her hair in my hand, and brought the knife to it, gently at first and then harder and harder. Luna wrenched away.

"Ouch!" she cried. "Don't pull so hard!"

"Well, this is a butter knife," I said practically. "I don't believe it will cut hair—it will barely cut butter. I think you'll have to pull your hair out by the roots if you want to remove it. And then you'll be bald, like Lord Edouard. Everyone will laugh at you, and you'll never get a husband!" I smiled, to let her know I was teasing. But she wasn't in the mood for a joke.

She grabbed the knife back from me, fuming. "I don't want a husband. I'm not like you, always mooning about marriage and wedding dresses. I want to do things! Instead, we're locked up here. Look at Mama— her life is so dreary. I couldn't bear it if that were my fate!"

"You know Mama isn't well," I reminded her. "She needs peace and quiet. And I don't believe she thinks her life is dreary. *I* don't think it's dreary. She's a queen, after all. You'll marry a prince and be a queen too when you grow up, and I will be queen here. That's important and interesting enough for me." Our parents had no son to inherit the kingdom, so it would be mine someday. Despite my offhand words, the idea had always terrified me. I couldn't imagine being queen and ruling my subjects. How could I face all those strangers, listen to their problems, and dispense wisdom and justice as Papa did?

Ignoring me, Luna got up and moved around the kitchen, opening drawers and cabinets and then slamming them shut in annoyance. "Why are there no real knives in our kitchen?" she demanded. "No pruning shears in the garden shed, no scissors to cut flowers—or hair? Why don't our guards have lances or swords? Why is there nothing sharp in the whole palace?"

"That's how it has always been, and you know it." I was surprised by her intensity. "Maybe Mama and Papa hid all the blades when you were born, fearing the damage you could do with a sharp instrument!"

Frustrated and angry, Luna raised the butter knife and tried to plunge it into the kitchen table, but its dull edge simply scratched the wood, and the knife bounced out of her hand, hitting a jar of honey and knocking it off the table to the floor. The jar shattered on the tiles, splattering honey on walls and floor and even on Luna's skirt. She bent down to grab a large, curved shard of the broken glass.

"Ah! This will do it," she said triumphantly.

"Luna, stop!" I cried in distress. "You know we're not permitted to touch anything sharp!"

She brought the shard, dripping with honey, to her hair and sliced. A curl fell to the ground. I reached out to stop her, but she dodged away, still cutting. I flinched as I saw the glass pierce her finger. She grimaced at the sight of blood, but she didn't stop. Oh, Mama would never forgive me for letting this happen!

Luna sliced through her hair again and again, leaving her locks scattered on the floor as she darted away from me. I chased her around the table, and she laughed and shrieked, overturning chairs and knocking a loaf of bread to the ground. I grabbed for her, but she danced out of my reach. Finally I just stood and watched helplessly as she chopped.

When not a single strand long enough to cut remained, Luna put the shard of glass down on the table. "There," she said. But her voice sounded a little uncertain. Her hands were streaked with honey and the blood that still dripped from her wounded finger. Clumps of hair stuck to her dress. Her gleeful expression began to fade.

"What have you done?" I whispered.

"Yes," Cook said from the doorway, "what on earth have you done now, Princess Luna?"

Cook's broad form filled the door, and her eyes were wide with shock. Her face, usually pink from constant exposure to the steam that rose from cook pots and the heat from the kitchen fires, was now strawberry red with alarm as she took in the chaos of her kitchen, which she always kept spotlessly clean.

"Princess, you're hurt!" she cried, seeing Luna's shorn head and the streaks of blood on her dress. "I'll get your mother."

"No!" Luna and I exclaimed together, exchanging an anxious glance.

"Please, don't bother the queen," I pleaded. "You'll only upset her needlessly. It's nothing—no more than a scratch. We were just . . ." But it was too late. Cook had spun on her heel and was treading heavily down the hallway. I could hear her mounting the stairs, muttering to herself.

"Help me clean this up," Luna begged frantically.

I looked about, dismayed. How had my sister done such damage in so short a time? We could never clean it before our parents came. "Oh, Luna," I said in despair, "we don't have a chance. And Papa will blame me."

I wanted to leave her there to face the consequences

alone, but I couldn't. She took my hand meekly in her sticky hand, and we stood still amid the wreckage. It felt as if we waited for hours, but I'm sure it was really only a few minutes. The sound of boots clattered down the stairs and along the hall, and then our father was in the room.

Papa glanced at me and then stared at Luna with his piercing dark eyes, speechless. Behind him came my mother, her brow creased with worry. She drew up abruptly when she saw the state of the kitchen—the honey smeared about, the hair-littered floor, the broken glass.

Then the smooth skin of Mama's face went as white as parchment. "The blood . . . ," she whispered. Her azure eyes were full of terror, as if she had seen a ghost or a monster. I wanted to tell her that Luna wasn't truly hurt, but I couldn't bring myself to speak. How could a haircut—even one as ragged as my sister's—make her so fearful?

And then, to my horror, Mama put her delicate, bejeweled hand to her chest and gracefully crumpled to the floor.

2

Of a Story
and a Spell

I screamed when Mama fainted, but Luna just
stood there, shorn like a boy, dripping blood
and honey. My cry brought the servants running, and then there was a huge commotion.

In a moment Mama's eyes fluttered open. Papa
raised her from the floor and helped her to a chair as
Cook and Jacquelle, the serving maid, fanned her and
offered her water and wine. Mama's dress was ruined, of
course, from the sticky honey that oozed everywhere. I
crouched beside her chair and took her ice-cold hands.

"Luna's not hurt, Mama," I said swiftly. "It was just

a little cut from the broken glass. You see, it isn't even bleeding anymore." I glared at Luna, and obediently she held out her hand to show the wound.

"And you?" My mother's voice trembled.

"Me? I'm fine!"

"Was . . . was there anyone else here?" The color began to return to Mama's face. She gazed around the kitchen, her eyes wide and frightened.

I was confused. "Anyone else? Why, no. It was just Luna and me. She got it into her head to cut her hair, and I couldn't stop her."

Finally Luna spoke. "I'm sorry, Mama," she said humbly. "I didn't mean to worry you."

Papa's expression darkened at her words. "Why is it, child, that you never mean the trouble you cause? Why would you do such an impulsive, foolish thing?"

Luna swallowed hard, and I felt a bit sorry for her. Papa's anger was rare, but when it came, we all felt its strength.

"I wasn't thinking," she admitted, looking down at the floor. "I was . . . oh, I don't know. I was bored, I suppose. I was so tired of my hair, and of everything. It's always the same here! Nothing ever changes. I wanted something to happen, so I made something happen." She sounded just a little bit proud then, and I frowned at her.

Papa shook his head, his fury gone as quickly as it had come. He could never stay angry with Luna for long. He didn't even punish her after the time she built a fire in the stable to roast chestnuts and very nearly burned it down. If my horse had been harmed, I would never have forgiven her. But Papa pardoned her whenever she cried and apologized and smiled at him through her tears.

"And why did you not stop your sister, Aurora?" Papa asked me.

I gulped. "I tried. I did try."

"She did!" Luna defended me. "She ran after me, but I was faster."

Did Papa's mouth twitch in a smile? "I am not surprised." His voice was stern, but his eyes twinkled at me, and I breathed a sigh of relief.

"Are you feeling stronger, Mama?" I said, chafing her hands to warm them. "Why did you faint? Luna's hair will grow back before long. And Cook can clean the mess."

"Oh, Daughter . . ." Mama's voice was so unexpectedly sad that I felt tears come to my eyes. "It was not her hair. It was the blood—the pierced finger. You do not know. . . ."

"Do not know what?" Luna piped up. "Why should a cut finger frighten you so? What *is* it?"

Mama looked at Papa, and he gazed back at her in silence. There was something strange in the air between them that made my heart beat faster.

"It is time, my dear," Papa finally said gently, and after a moment Mama nodded.

"Time for what?" Luna was wild with curiosity. "Time for *what*?" she asked again. Papa put his finger across his lips, glancing at the servants who were still in the kitchen, sponging the floor and table and walls.

"We will take luncheon in the conservatory," Papa told Cook, helping Mama up from the chair. We followed them out of the kitchen in silence, Luna dancing with eagerness.

"Aurora," Mama said to me when we reached the main floor of the palace, "take your sister up to her bedchamber and help her clean herself. Luna, you will have to bathe—only hot water and lemon soap will get the honey out. Change your dress. Come to us when you are finished." Her voice was stronger now, and uncharacteristically severe. I curtsied to her, pulling Luna into a curtsy too, and we scurried up the stairs.

The upstairs maid, Florine, who was not much older than I, brought hot water to pour into the copper tub in Luna's room. She stared outright at Luna's cropped hair as she prepared the bath.

"Heavens, Princess, you are a sight!" she said

impudently. "You look like a boy in girl's dress. It will take a year or more for your hair to grow back!"

Luna snorted, peeling off her ruined dress and stepping into the steaming bath. "I don't want it to grow back," she declared firmly. "I like it very well just like this."

"Well!" Florine, scandalized, pursed her lips and shook her head. "No prince will come calling for a bald-headed princess!"

As expected, my sister was not displeased with this idea. "That's one problem solved," she noted as Florine hurried from the room. "I said I didn't want to marry a prince—and now no prince will have me."

I scrubbed her hair, rather more roughly than needed, with a sea sponge. "You may change your mind someday," I pointed out, and squeezed the sponge so that water cascaded over her face and into her mouth, quieting her. "You're only nine—you have plenty of time to think about princes."

She shook her head violently, spattering me. "I will not," she retorted with certainty.

I soaped and rinsed, soaped and rinsed her hair. Finally the honey was gone, and Luna stepped out and dried herself, rubbing her head hard with a towel. The hair sprang into tight curls around her head like a little brown cap. Uneven in places, it still was . . .

surprisingly becoming. She did not look like a boy at all, but like a pretty, boyish girl.

"Why," I said, "it looks rather nice!"

Luna pulled on a shift and ran to the mirror. The short curls revealed the heart shape of her face and made her hazel eyes seem much bigger and darker.

"Mama won't faint at this, will she?" she said, smiling at her reflection.

"Well, I don't think she'll be pleased." I was still worried about Mama's swoon. "Princesses don't have short hair."

"This one does," Luna said, turning so she could see her hair in the back.

I took a gown from the wardrobe and held it out. "Put this on, quickly. We must get back to Mama and Papa."

But Luna would not be rushed. "No more combs or brushes! No more braids or ribbons! No more scorched hair from overheated curling irons!" She twirled before the mirror.

"Hurry up," I insisted, tossing the gown to her. "Or I will go and learn whatever secret they are keeping without you!"

Dry and dressed at last, she ran down the stairs and into the conservatory ahead of me. The room was glassed in on all sides and warmed by the sun even on cold days. Flowers and greenery that would not grow outdoors in our windy, bitter climate flourished here. It was Mama's favorite room in the palace, and mine as well.

Mama lay on a chaise in a fresh dress with a cool cloth on her forehead. A small table had been set nearby, and three other chairs were pulled up to it. I sat, tugging Luna down beside me. She tapped her feet anxiously as Papa paced the room, clearly upset. Jacquelle finished ladling soup into our bowls and left us.

Even then Papa did not speak. He sat in his chair and sipped his soup. I had the feeling that he was doing this very deliberately, to punish Luna by making her wait. He would not look at her. Mama, though, motioned Luna to sit beside her on the chaise. She ran her hand over Luna's damp curls.

"It suits you, child," she said. Luna beamed, then jumped up and went back to her seat to start on her soup.

I could hardly believe it. After all the frenzy—the broken glass, the haircut, the mess, and Mama fainting— was Luna merely to be complimented? I had to grit my teeth to keep my anger from showing. I knew there was nothing I could do about it. I wondered, as I often had before, what would have happened if I had been the one to misbehave. But I wouldn't have. I never did.

I pushed down my exasperation and asked, "Mama, what is it? Why did you faint? You are not . . . ill, are you?"

"Oh, no, dearest," Mama replied. "It is nothing like that."

"Then tell us, please!"

Mama sighed deeply and looked at Papa as she had in the kitchen, as if for guidance.

"It is your story, my love." He took her trembling hand in his. "You must tell it."

"Then I shall," she said simply, and she began.

"I have never told you much about my life. It is . . . not a happy story. I was one of two children born to my parents. My brother was very much older than I, handsome and full of life."

Luna dropped her soup spoon with a clatter, and I gaped. Mama had a brother? There'd never been even a hint of any uncle. Why had we never met him?

Mama ignored our astonishment. "My parents adored him, but still they longed for a daughter to pamper and indulge. For many years it seemed their wish would not be granted, so when at last I was born, they were jubilant. All of our relatives, and all the important lords and ladies and dignitaries for many miles around, were invited to my christening. Of course I was an infant, so I do not remember what happened.

But when I was your age, Aurora, my mother told me the story."

Something in her tone made me shiver. I had a feeling that this tale would not end well.

Chapter Two continues . . .

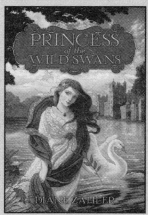